permanent rose

Also by Hilary McKay

Indigo's Star

Saffy's Angel

Dolphin Luck

Caddy Ever After

The Amber Cat

Dog Friday

The Exiles

The Exiles at Home

The Exiles in Love

Margaret K. McElderry Books

permanent rose

HILARY McKAY

Aladdin Paperbacks
New York London Toronto Sydney

To Jennifer Luithlen,
who is so much more
than a fantastic agent

This book is a work of fiction. Any references to historical events, real people, or real locales are used fictitiously. Other names, characters, places, and incidents are the product of the author's imagination, and any resemblance to actual events or locales or persons, living or dead, is entirely coincidental.

ALADDIN PAPERBACKS
An imprint of Simon & Schuster Children's Publishing Division
1230 Avenue of the Americas, New York, NY 10020

Also available in a Margaret K. McElderry Books
Designed by Kristin Smith
The text of this book was set in Melior.
Manufactured in the United States of America
First published in Great Britain in 2005 by Hodder Children's Books
First Aladdin Paperbacks edition December 2006
10 9 8 7 6 5 4 3 2 1
Library of Congress Cataloging-in-Publication Data
McKay, Hilary.
Permanent Rose / Hilary McKay.—1st ed.
p. cm.
Summary: While trying to reconnect with her friend Tom, who has returned to the United States without leaving a forwarding address, eight-year-old Rose inadvertently discovers the identity of her adopted sister Saffy's father.
[1. Self-confidence—Fiction. 2. Friendship—Fiction. 3. Fathers—Fiction. 4. Brothers and sisters—Fiction. 5. Family life—England—Fiction. 6. England—Fiction.] I. Title. PZ7.M4786574Pe 2005 [Fic]—dc20
2004025891
ISBN-13: 978-1-4169-0372-7 (hc.)
ISBN-10: 1-4169-0372-0 (hc.)
ISBN-13: 978-1-4169-2804-1 (pbk.)
ISBN-10: 1-4169-2804-9 (pbk.)

Praise for *Saffy's Angel*

★"A sheer delight." —*Booklist*, starred review
★"A memorable portrait." —*Publishers Weekly*, starred review
★"Wonderfully descriptive." —*School Library Journal*, starred review
★"Hilary McKay . . . made me want to read it all in one sitting." —*Horn Book*, starred review

Winner of the Whitbread Award
An ALA Notable Book
A *Child* Magazine Best Book
A *Boston Globe-Horn Book* Honor Book
A *Horn Book* Fanfare Selection
A *School Library Journal* Best Book
A *Booklist* Editors' Choice
A *Center for Children's Books Bulletin* Blue Ribbon Selection
A *Publishers Weekly* Best Children's Book

Praise for *Indigo's Star*

★ "Readers . . . will wish they could be adopted by the Cassons." —*Kirkus Reviews*, starred review
★ "Readers will love revisiting the chaotic-but-loving Casson household." —*School Library Journal*, starred review
★ "An artful collection." —*Horn Book*, starred review
★ "The Cassons are as riotous and refreshing as ever." —*Publishers Weekly*, starred review

A Parents' Choice Silver Honor Book
A *Publishers Weekly* Best Children's Book
A *Kirkus Reviews* Editor's Choice
A *Horn Book* Fanfare Selection

Chapter One

DAVID TRAMPED ALONG THE ROAD TO THE CASSON HOUSE trying not to think too far ahead. In his pocket was a packet of banana-flavored chews. He had started his journey with three packets (watermelon, lime, and banana), but now only banana was left. Every few steps he unwrapped a fresh sweet and bundled it into his mouth. He did the unwrapping in his pocket and the bundling in one quick furtive movement that looked like a yawn.

It was the last week of the school summer holidays, late August, and smotheringly hot. David was on his way to visit Indigo Casson, something he had been meaning to do all summer. The nearer he got to Indigo's house, the harder he chewed.

Chomp, chomp, chomp, went David, and then he accidentally gulped and swallowed before he had the next sweet unwrapped. For the first time since he had started out, his mouth was empty. Chewing had been David's way of stopping himself from thinking very hard. Now (and without any encouragement at all from David) his brain lurched into action.

What if Indigo's dad opens the door?

Please not him! prayed David as he fumbled with a particularly tight chew wrapper.

Indigo's father was an artist: Bill Casson. Artist.

It was hard to believe. He looked like someone from a TV ad for something very expensive. Sports cars. Or first class train travel. He did not look as if he had ever been near anything as messy as paint.

Two things about Indigo's father had alarmed David when they had met. The first was this inhuman cleanness. The second was the way he had glanced at David. As if David was someone he intended (for obvious reasons) to have nothing at all to do with. David, always aware of his lifetime's collection of guilty secrets struggling to escape, had been shocked at being seen through so quickly.

But Indigo's dad will be in London, David told himself, as he finally got the chew wrapper free at last. *He nearly always is in London.* David bit down comfortingly into a new sweet. *Good.*

Banana-flavored chews were the best. Watermelon were a little too exotic, and lime slightly sour. Banana were perfect. Except for being much too small. In a David-perfect world they would have been the size and shape of a smallish egg. And not wrapped.

I hope I don't see Indigo's mum, either, thought David, swallowing a chew whole to see if it hurt.

David did not actually know Indigo's mother; he did not know anyone's mother except his own. However, he assumed all mothers were more or less the same, and when he had stopped choking (it hurt), he loaded in a fresh new chew and made a plan.

If Indigo's mum answers the door, I'll run off!

The packet of sweets was no longer a packet. It was a stump submerged in wrappers. David absentmindedly scooped them out of his pocket as he trudged along and then suddenly turned back and began to scrabble them up again. Very recently (that day in fact) he had stopped being the sort of person who drops rubbish in the street. Now he was the sort of person who picks it up, and he was surprised at how different that felt. Extraordinarily noble, and embarrassingly grubby at the same time.

He kept a wary eye on Indigo's house as he collected his papers. An awful lot of girls lived there.

"How many sisters have you got?" he had once asked Indigo.

"Three," Indigo had replied, and then, reconsidering, "No, two really."

"Don't you know?"

Indigo said of course he knew, and he listed his sisters for David.

"Caddy. She's at college in London, but she's home for the summer."

"She's grown-up then," pronounced David. He did not like grown-ups. "Grown-up!" he repeated disconsolately.

Indigo said he supposed so. Caddy, scatty, golden-haired, last seen tearfully designing a gravestone for her most recent dead hamster, did not seem particularly grown-up.

"Caddy's the eldest," Indigo told David. "Then there's Saffron, but she's not really my sister; she's my cousin. She came to live with us ages ago when she was little, when her mother died. Her mother was my mother's sister, so we adopted her. Anyway, you know Saffron!"

David winced at the thought of Saffron, whom he knew only too well. She was fifteen, more than a year older than he and Indigo, clever, gorgeous, and ruthless. She and her best friend had once invaded the boys' washroom and attacked the leader of the most vicious gang in the school. Her friend had guarded the door to stop anyone from escaping while Saffron had nearly pulled off the gang leader's head. Not one of his henchmen, including David, had dared raise a finger to stop her.

What if Saffron opened the door?

David unwrapped the whole of the rest of the packet of chews and pushed them into his mouth all together. They fitted easily. Only two tiny yellow triangles of dribble at the corners of his lips showed that they were there at all.

Saffron'll have forgotten about me by now, thought David, who was a hopeful person.

The last of Indigo's sisters was very young, not quite nine, dark-haired and white-faced, completely different from Caddy and Saffron. Nothing about her was alarmingly good-looking, or grown-up, or tough. Her name was Rose. Permanent Rose.

• • •

"Permanent Rose!" said people whenever they heard Rose's name for the first time. "What kind of name is Permanent Rose?"

"It's my kind of name," said Rose.

"Is it a joke?"

That was the question everyone asked.

Everyone.

Even Rose's own father had asked it once.

Rose could just remember the huge indignant fuss he had made when she was four years old and her father had finally discovered that her amusing pet name was not, as he had always supposed, an amusing pet name at all.

"Permanent Rose!" he had repeated over and over again. "*Permanent Rose!* No!"

He had been filling in a form for a new passport, putting on all the children's names, so that they could travel with him. "Just in case," said Bill, who always did things just in case. Caddy, Saffron, and Indigo were already safely listed, and then he came to Rose. She was hanging around watching every move he made, the way she always did when he was home.

"Your turn, Rosy Pose!" he had said, smiling down at her.

Then he picked up Rose's birth certificate, which he had never happened to see before. And there it was.

Permanent Rose.

"Eve, *darling*!" said Bill (Eve was Rose's mother). *"Darling!"* repeated Bill (very indignant and far from amused). "What *were* you thinking of?"

Eve, who was also an artist, had been thinking of the color that painters use: permanent rose. A clear, warm color that glows with its own lively brightness, no matter how thinly spread. A color that does not fade. There had been a permanent rose–colored sky on the morning that Rose was born.

Rose had arrived into the world a lot earlier than anyone had expected her to do, and from the absolute beginning she had seemed very unthrilled about the prospect of having to stay. She had been like a visitor who hovers on a doorstep, wondering if it is worth the bother of actually coming in. People had sent flowers to Eve, but not baby toys or little clothes. It did not seem that Rose intended to be around long enough to need such things.

Eve knew quite well why she only got flowers. That was why one afternoon she had slipped out of the hospital and gone all by herself across the town to register the latest Casson's defiant name. Permanent Rose.

"Permanent Rose," said Tom, "is the coolest name on the planet!"

That had been back in the spring, when Tom had first arrived into Rose's life. He was an American boy, the same age as Indigo, who had spent the spring term at Indigo's school. Tom and Indigo and Rose had become best friends. It had not seemed to matter that Rose was only eight years old.

"More than eight," said Rose. "Nearly nine."

"Darling Rose, even nearly-nine-year-olds don't fall in love," said forgetful Caddy.

Caddy tried very hard to comfort Rose when Tom went away. It was not an easy job. It was like trying to comfort a small, unhappy tiger.

"Who said anything about falling in love?" growled Rose crossly. "Falling! Falling is by accident! I didn't fall in anything!"

"Oh. Right. Sorry, Rose."

"And I am *definitely* not in love!"

"No. Okay, Rosy Pose. Sorry about that, too."

Rose, who was sitting on Caddy's bed, hunched her knees up under her chin, turned her back, and sighed. Caddy sighed too. The room became very quiet until Rose asked suddenly, "What is the name for it when you are trying to paint a picture and you haven't any red? Or blue? Or yellow? When you finish a jigsaw and a piece is not there? When Indigo's guitar loses a string and a whole lot of notes are suddenly missing?"

"Oh, Rose!"

"Is there a name for it?"

"Incomplete." Caddy reached across and rubbed her little sister's drooping shoulders. "You would call it incomplete."

"Would you?"

"I think so. Is that how you felt when Tom went away?"

"Not at first," said Rose.

"The *coolest* name on the planet!"

Tom had said it again, the very last time that Rose had seen him. "*Permanent Rose!* Oh, yes! So what am I going to do without you, Permanent Rose?"

"You don't have to do without me."

"I have to go back to America."

"I'll still be here."

Indigo leaned over and scuffled Rose's hair with a music magazine he was holding. Tom did not reply at all, just grinned and bent a little lower over his guitar. There was a good feeling in the air, the way that happens in a place when all the people there are friends with each other. If Rose could have stopped time right then, she would have, but she couldn't. Time went on, and Tom went away.

This was how it had happened, that for Indigo and Rose, the summer began with an ending. Tom was gone. He had gone home to America because his baby sister was seriously ill. Earlier in the year he had fled to England to escape her. Now, it seemed, she might escape him instead.

Ever since the night Tom had left, Indigo and Rose had waited for news.

Hour by hour, and then day by day.

No news came.

Nothing.

Tom, comrade and companion-in-arms to Indigo,

troubadour, jester, and storyteller to Rose, sent no word at all.

He did not telephone, and he did not write. He did not communicate in any way. They had not heard a word from him.

It was not so bad for Indigo; he was older, and he had Tom's old guitar to learn to play, and he had a larger supply of patience than most people. He said, "Tom knows where we are. And it hasn't been that long."

It seemed long to Rose. The summer holidays had passed in a blur of heat and waiting. Tom's absence haunted her. In town she would catch glimpses of someone with a walk like his, and for a moment be certain that he was back. At night she often dreamed of him, stifling nightmares of noncommunication. Two or three times she struggled right out of these dreams and down the stairs to the kitchen, convinced she had heard the telephone ring.

"It is two o'clock in the morning, Rose!" said Eve, hugging her, the third time this happened. "And anyway, we cannot even hear the telephone upstairs, unless all the doors are open."

"I know."

"Come on back to bed then. You should be asleep."

"Can we leave all the doors open?"

"Do you fall asleep waiting for the telephone to ring, Rose?"

Rose nodded.

"No wonder you have nightmares," said Eve, but after that all the doors were left open, and Rose's nightmares stopped.

The nightmares stopped, but Rose's waiting did not stop. She still jumped every time the telephone rang, or when she saw a familiar gray jacket in the street. She waited impatiently for the post every morning.

"Do you know how long Tom has been gone *now*?" she asked Indigo that last Monday morning of the summer holidays.

"It must be more than five weeks."

"It has been five weeks and two days," said Rose.

"Oh."

"Five weeks, two days, and about eleven hours. Why are you smiling?"

"Because your math is so good."

"It wasn't math, it was counting," said Rose.

• • •

When David rang the doorbell of Indigo's house, Tom had been gone five weeks and two days and about twelve hours.

At the sound of the bell Rose jumped. Something inside her lifted, and then dropped a little too far. As if her heart had unexpectedly missed a step on a stairway.

She rushed to the door and dragged it open, but of course it was not Tom. It was only David, smelling (as usual) of sweets and sweat and looking redder and hotter than it was natural for any human being to look, even in the middle of a heat wave.

Rose gazed at him with dislike, which did not upset David because he did not notice.

"I've come to see Indigo," he announced.

"He's in the garden," snapped Rose, and shut the door as quickly as she had pulled it open.

David was never very fast at taking in information, especially when it was hurled at him by white-faced little girls with hardly any clothes on. So he remained where he was, huge, sticky, panting a little, and he was still there when Rose pulled the door open again and demanded, "Would you like to be tattooed?"

"Yes," said David, who longed more than anything to be tattooed, pierced, studded, thin, witty, swift, and effortlessly cool, and was none of these things.

"Oh, good."

Then David noticed that Rose was holding a bunch of ballpoint pens in one hand and an old-fashioned steel-nibbed pen in the other, that various parts of her body were beautifully patterned in red and blue ink, and that she was looking speculatively at his own large, pink unadorned arms.

"I've been practicing designs all week," he heard her say. "And I've just found this pen, and I'm sure it's sharp enough to do the real thing. . . . I don't suppose it hurts much . . . Come back!"

But David had already gone, fleeing in horror around the side of the house, past the overgrown fig tree whose dark leaves rubbed and rustled as if there were animals among them, and across to the patch of rough grass and guinea-pig hutches that the Casson family called a garden.

Rose should have called, "Stop!"—thus saving him. But she didn't.

There was no shade at all in the Cassons' garden, and that day the sunlight was so bright it was like a sound in the air: the jangling echo that might come after an enormous gong had been struck. It added to the dazed, alarmed confusion in David's head, so that he could not seem to think or see very clearly.

At first there did not appear to be anyone about. Then David became aware of a screen that had been made of guinea-pig hutches and draped blankets.

"Indigo?" he called, and blundered forward and nearly died of fright.

Except for a recent period (spent as a random but violent thug), David had had a very sheltered existence. Apart from Rose, he had never voluntarily spoken to a girl in his life. He was not a bit prepared for the fearsome (and yet ravishing) sight of Saffron, entirely naked except for dark glasses and flip-flops, industriously sunbathing among the guinea pigs.

"Rose?" asked Saffron sleepily, lifting her head. Then she shoved back her sunglasses to look properly, and her eyes glinted with silver sparks and she said coldly, "Oh. Not Rose. David. Get out. Go."

David did not go. He did not move. He could not. He wanted to say, "Rose sent me here," but he could not speak because his mouth was hanging open, and he could not summon up the strength to get it shut. He was now so feverishly hot that he thought he must be terribly ill. It occurred to him that if he died right then, it would be simultaneously much too late and much too soon.

"Indigo!" called Saffron very loudly. "Come and take this boy away before his eyes fall out!"

From another screened-off corner that David had not noticed, Indigo's head emerged, wearing a set of headphones. Indigo did not seem to be at all disturbed by the presence of naked females. He was not; he was used to them, having lived with them all his life. Pulling his headphones off as he spoke, he said quite calmly, "Oh, David. Hi. Didn't see you!"

David lifted a shaking hand and pointed helplessly at Saffron.

"Indigo," said Saffron furiously. "If you do not take this boy away, I will get up and *chase* him away!"

Indigo grinned suddenly and said, "Come on, David! Let's go to the house! I think you've probably seen enough!"

Then at last David moved, a lurching step backward that brought him into collision with a homemade guinea-pig hutch, all sharp corners and rusty catches and wobbly legs. He fell down on top of it, cutting himself in several places, annoying the resident very much, and showering Saffron in hay, sawdust, and guinea-pig droppings. Behind him Rose said in a cold little voice, "It was nice before you came."

"It was nice before you came," repeated Rose, and she looked at the thick line of dark blood now trickling from David's elbow and added, "Yuck."

David hastily blotted the offending gore with his sleeve, and then, anxious to repair the damage he had caused, picked up the guinea-pig hutch, hesitated for a moment, glanced at Saffron's gleaming but guinea-piggy back, rubbed his perspiring hands on the front of his shirt, and then bravely plunged forward, clearly intending to personally decontaminate her at once.

"Touch me and I'll slay you," remarked Saffron as, just in time, Indigo grabbed David from behind.

"This way!" he ordered, and began towing him toward the house, and by the time they had reached the doorstep, David had come back to his senses again.

"I'm sorry!" he called huskily in the general direction of the silent garden.

He waited, but no answer came. Obviously he did not rate high enough for even an indignant reply.

"Don't worry," said Indigo, confirming his feeling of utter unimportance. "She'll soon forget! Wait in the kitchen while I fetch some Band-Aids and stuff. Look after him, Rose!"

Rose looked after David by glaring at him and asking awkward questions.

"Why'd you come here?"

"To see Indigo."

"You were in that gang. You used to beat him up."

"I'm his friend now," said David.

David had a very basic understanding of life. If you were someone's friend, he thought, you came to see them. You were on their side. Their battles were your battles. The things they cared about were the things you cared about. If you were not someone's friend, you were their enemy. You would probably at some time find yourself beating them up. To become someone's friend, even if you had been their enemy, was quite straightforward. You said, 'I'm your friend.' It was possible to switch from being an enemy to a friend that easily.

Until this summer that was how David had always understood the world to be, but lately the uncomfortable feeling had been growing on him that things were not quite as simple as he had supposed.

Rose said, "I remember everything you did to Indigo. And Tom."

David's eyes turned down in shame. And also in disappointment, because he had secretly hoped that the time he and the gang had spent tormenting Indigo and Tom had been conveniently forgotten by everyone concerned. Sometimes he almost convinced himself that this was true, simply because it *had* to be true, or else how could he get through the days? Other times he thought it never would be forgotten. He did not see how it could be, when he could not forget it himself.

It made it very difficult to be friends with Indigo.

"You were one of the ones who helped stuff him down a toilet," Rose continued relentlessly. "So I think you've got a big cheek coming around here and saying you're his friend! *Tom* was his friend! Not you!"

"I know," agreed David. "But Tom's gone now."

"He hasn't gone, he's just in America! And anyway, even if he had gone, you wouldn't do instead!"

"So I thought," continued David after waiting patiently for Rose to stop shouting, "Tom's gone. And it's school again soon. And me and Indigo can be friends next term. We were going to be earlier anyway. We were going to go skateboarding—only the park got vandalized . . . Were you joking about that tattooing? Do you really know how?"

"You cut slits. And rub in ink."

"Crikey. Is that what you've done to yourself?"

"Of course not! This is just ballpoint."

"It looks like real. It's very good."

Rose shrugged, but inside she felt rather alarmed. David's approval was the last thing she wanted. She escaped upstairs to her tiny bedroom, planning to have a very hard think about her tattoos. None of her family liked them. Even her mother, the least critical person in the world, had said (as more and more of Rose became blotted out by blue and red ink), "I wish you wouldn't do it." This had been very surprising, especially as Eve herself had a lovely branching tree on the top of one arm, and the words *Move Over* in curly italics on her stomach.

"But you don't know how much I wish I hadn't!" she had said when Rose pointed this out. "Anyway, think what Daddy would say!"

"Who cares what Daddy would say?" Rose had asked. She had a very loving and hating relationship with her father. His artistic London life, with his artistic London studio and newly-admitted-to artistic London girlfriend named Samantha, made him seem very far away to Rose. The more often he told Rose how important she was, the more she suspected that he could do perfectly well without her.

Things were changing too fast in Rose's world. Her father was gone, and Samantha had arrived. Tom had vanished. Indigo's enemies appeared at the door and announced that they had become his friends. Caddy, who once had been hardly ever sad, was now hardly ever happy. . . .

Caddy could not do without Rose. She called out to her as soon as she heard her come upstairs. Rose found her busy ransacking the tremendous clutter of the bedroom she shared with Saffron, in search of her newly acquired engagement ring.

"I've lost that awful diamond again!" she said when Rose appeared at the door. "You are small enough to get under beds, Rosy Pose! Come and help me look!"

"You shouldn't keep taking it off!" said Rose, obediently getting down on her hands and knees.

"Well, I can't wear it all the time, can I? Like a dog collar! Or a ball and chain!"

"Don't you want to marry Michael?"

"Of course I do!"

"Good."

"Although I do think it's a lot to exchange for one miserable diamond."

"What is?"

"Me."

Rose reversed out from under the bed, sat back on her heels, and looked thoughtfully at Caddy. "I like Michael," she said.

"I *adore* Michael!" said Caddy hastily. "But I must admit he was more adorable still when he didn't care so much about me! And I wish he'd stop talking about dates!"

"What sort of dates?"

"Wedding day dates!" said Caddy, shaking out shoes in the bottom of her wardrobe. "For next year when I finish college. Poor darling! Bonkers! Oh! Here it is! In one of those horrible clog things! Do you really think I should marry Michael, Rosy Pose?"

"Yes, I do," said Rose at once. "I think you should marry Michael and live in a house very close by and do loads of cooking and have a lot of children . . ."

Caddy had just pushed her engagement ring onto

her finger, but now, looking absolutely appalled at this vision of her future, she pulled it off again.

". . . and I could come and baby-sit," continued Rose, not noticing. "It would be brilliant. I should always know where you were . . . Why are you putting your ring in that box?"

"To keep it safe," said Caddy, and then to change the subject she asked, "Who is that I can hear downstairs with Indigo?"

"Oh." Rose, who had cheered up at the thought of having Caddy reliably trapped close by forever, became gloomy again. "It's horrible-rubbish-David."

"Who is horrible-rubbish-David?"

"He's that fat boy who smells of sweets. He used to help beat Indigo up."

"What's he doing here?"

"He thinks now that Tom's gone he can be Indigo's friend. Instead of Tom."

"Ridiculous!" said Caddy robustly. "Totally not possible! Or is it?"

"Nobody can be instead of Tom," said Rose.

Chapter Two

THE MORNING GREW HOTTER AND HOTTER. SAFFRON'S BEST friend, Sarah, arrived in her wheelchair (which she discarded along with most of her clothes) and joined Saffron in the garden.

Sarah came from one of the big houses down the road. Once she had been a lonely person, but now the Cassons' muddled, welcoming home was as friendly to her as her own. She was very fond of the whole family, including Eve and Bill. It no longer surprised her that Eve sometimes spent whole days and nights painting and dozing in the garden shed, and she got on very well with Bill, who liked fast cars as much as she did and sent her Ferrari magazines from London.

Most of all, however, she cared about Caddy, Saffron, Indigo, and Rose. To Sarah they were the brother and sisters she had always wanted.

Like everyone else who had known Tom, Sarah

was waiting for news. The first question she asked as she came into the garden was, "Has anyone heard anything from America yet?"

"Not a word," answered Saffron, moving over to make room for her on the rug. "Nothing. Better put your top back on, by the way. That awful David's about."

"Not David-the-enormous-vegetable-henchman?"

"That's the one."

"I wondered why you were wearing so many clothes!" said Sarah, pulling her own back on as fast as possible. "I'd have brought a coat or two if I'd known! Fancy being ogled by David!"

"It was accidental ogling!" Saffron told her. "I don't think he's into bare skin. He saw too much of mine and collapsed onto the guinea-pig hutch. Blood and sawdust everywhere . . . Sarah, you will roast if you get right under that rug!"

"Better roasted than ogled," said Sarah firmly. "Collapsed! I don't think so! Probably pounced and fell over! So anyway, nothing from Tom? He's forgotten us then. Poor Indigo. Poor Rose. I thought they'd stay friends forever and ever."

"Callous beyond belief," said Saffron.

Saffron and Sarah had a way of summoning up a subject, considering it, judging it, and dismissing it, all in a few moments. After they had agreed that Tom was callous beyond belief to abandon Indigo and Rose so completely, they went on to:

David (Wouldn't trust him)
Global warming (Gorgeous if this is it)
Eve's summer job at the hospital (It gets her out of the shed)
Guinea pigs (No)
Rose's fake tattooing (It's a phase)
Bill and his new girlfriend, Samantha

They slowed down when they reached Bill and Samantha.

"Do you remember how Rose used to write him scary letters to try and make him come home?" asked Saffron. "I bet he stays in London more than ever now."

She sounded so untroubled that Sarah looked at her in surprise.

"I should hate it if my father dumped Mum and me and never came home!" she said.

"You've forgotten," said Saffron. "You've forgotten like everyone forgets! He's not my father."

"No, I didn't forget! But what's the difference? You've lived with Eve and Bill since you were three years old, Saffy! Indigo can't remember a time when you weren't here. Rose wasn't even born when you first came. Bill suddenly producing Samantha *can't* feel any different to you than it does to the others."

Saffron did not try to argue, but presently she said, "Sarah?"

"Mmmm?"

"I must have a real father somewhere."

Sarah was so startled that she crawled out from under the rug and stared at Saffron.

"I suppose you must!"

"Do you think it matters that I don't know who he is?"

"Not a bit," said Sarah at once, and very firmly in case Saffron was feeling insecure.

"Don't you think I ought to know who I am?"

"You are Saffron." Sarah pulled the rug back over herself again. "Nothing can change that."

After that the garden was quiet for a long time.

"I suppose you could find out who he was if you really wanted to," said Sarah eventually.

Then the garden was silent again.

David's approval had been too insulting. Rose decided that her tattoos would have to go. However, deciding they would have to go and actually making them disappear were two different things. Rose scrubbed and scrubbed but remained almost as brightly patterned in red and blue as ever. Eventually she gave up and went to get help from Saffron and Sarah. They prescribed nail polish remover and Saffron went indoors to hunt for some.

"Saffy told me that there was still no news from Tom," Sarah remarked sympathetically to Rose as they waited together. "Poor Rosy Pose. He's a barbarian!"

"He is not!" said Rose, more for the sake of arguing than because she had anything against barbarians.

"Who is not what?" inquired Saffron, returning just then with her hands full of bottles.

"Tom a barbarian," Rose told her.

"Tom!" said Saffron scornfully, unscrewing a bottle and slopping the contents onto cotton wool.

"Keep still, Rose, and I'll get that star off your cheek! You know, you should forget about Tom. Every time you remember him, you should tell yourself straight afterward, 'Forgotten!' Shouldn't she, Sarah?"

"Only thing to do," agreed Sarah airily, beginning on a blue butterfly on Rose's left shoulder. "Hey, this stuff really works! Have a go at your knees, Rose, while I finish this arm! Yes, about Tom. It is a pity that you ever got so fond of him in the first place. It's nearly always disastrous . . ."

Sarah paused, obviously remembering the last person she had become too disastrously fond of.

"Yes, well," she began again, "never again! In fact, Saffron and I have decided that the best thing to do with most boys (not Indigo, of course!) is to cultivate a heart of stone. . . ."

"What does that mean?"

"Well, basically dump them first!" said Sarah. "Instead of the horrible, humiliating other way around! So, Saffy's going to give a time limit (three weeks max and off they'll go!), and I shall rank my feelings for them on a scale of one to ten (David would be zero, for instance, and Justin Timberlake, eight), and anyone causing anything over six point five will be immediately discontinued. . . . Would you rate Tom over six point five, Rosy Pose?"

"No one can make me do math at school," said Rose calmly, "and no one can make me do it at home, either. So! I've finished my legs. What about the rest of me? Am I nearly done?"

"More or less," said Saffron, looking at her critically. "Just a bit purplish, and that will have to wear off. I've just used the last drop of remover. I shall have to buy some more. Come on, let's go and find a mirror!"

Rose helped Saffron get Sarah to her feet, and they went indoors. There Rose inspected her new unembellished appearance, Saffron made sandwiches for lunch, and Sarah unpinned the artist's color chart from the kitchen wall and spread it out on the table. She hung over it, picking out the family names.

"There's Caddy! Cadmium gold. Eve *was* good at names! Here's Indigo. And here's the saffron yellow they added for you, Saffy (but saffron is a spice really). . . . It's so not fair that you were all called after colors and spices and I was called after a dead old lady!"

"What would you choose to be?" asked Rose, coming to look over her shoulder. "If you weren't called after a dead old lady?"

"Scarlet," said Sarah at once. "My favorite color! What would you choose, Rose, if you weren't Permanent Rose?"

"Nothing."

"If you *had* to change?"

Rose remembered Tom saying, "Permanent Rose is the coolest name on the planet." If Tom was a barbarian, Rose liked barbarians.

"I *wouldn't* change," she said.

After lunch Caddy went off to work at her pub, and Saffron and Sarah began getting together their swimming things. A new outdoor pool had opened just down the road, and there Sarah daily transformed into a mermaid.

"Come with us," they urged Rose, but she shook her head and disappeared upstairs until they were out of the way.

Indigo was in his room now; Rose could hear him pulling careful notes out of his old guitar, while the creak and drone of David's voice went on and on in the background. Saffron and Sarah would be gone for ages. Eve, who was working at the hospital, would not be home for hours and hours.

Sometimes, for no particular reason, Rose's spirits would rise, as if a breeze had lifted her high above the usual, consequential world. This was one of those times.

Permanent Rose, she thought, and slipped out of the house, past the fig tree, onto the empty sunny street, and then far along the street (where she was not allowed to go) until she reached the center of town. There the sunlight was dazzling off plate-glass windows, and the shadows were sharp and black, and the cobbled pavements seethed with people, and Rose slid between them, as anonymous as a little fish in a shoal.

Rose had a new hobby that summer. Shoplifting. It was a game she played.

Long ago Rose had received a birthday present she liked very much. It was a tube of long, thin wooden sticks of different colors. The challenge was to spill the sticks into a prickly pile and then lift them up, one by one, without disturbing any of the heap underneath. Sarah had called it Spillikins. Rose called it Pick-up Sticks, and she was very good at it.

Rose's shoplifting was almost the same game. The aim was to move an object, not a stick of course, but something small, like a chocolate bar, or a pencil sharpener maybe, without any disturbance. Without anyone noticing.

At first she had just moved little things within the shop, rearranging the shelves. That quickly grew too easy, so she started taking the things outside.

In Rose's mind this was not stealing because she did not keep the things. She never ate the sweets she picked up, nor took home the pencils, tiny notebooks, hair bobbles, or whatever it happened to be that day. Always, very soon after they had been taken, they would be left behind, tidily balanced on a rubbish bin perhaps, or on top of a low wall. Not thrown away but safely placed, the way passersby sometimes leave odd gloves or baby toys they find in the street for the owner to come back and collect.

This was Rose's game, private, skillful, and a little tingly. It really was shoplifting: She lifted things out of shops. Sometimes she played it when she was out with her mother (which was easy because Eve never noticed anything), now and then with Indigo (which was harder unless he went into one of his dreams), and once or twice when she was in town with Saffron and Sarah. This was the hardest of all; Saffron and Sarah's quest for retail perfection was assiduous and untiring. They never went into dreams.

Very rarely, when she could escape from home unnoticed (which was not allowed and not easy either), Rose played the shoplifting game by herself.

This was one of those times.

High overhead, the heat rose from the rooftops and rippled like water into the shining blue above. Below, the colored canvas of the market stalls hung heavy in the windless air. A tide of people surged and poured across the cobbled market and in and out of the shops all around. Rose let herself be carried by their movement, swirled into sudden pools of sunlight, dropped to drift for a while in shadowy alcoves, and then picked up again and rushed to somewhere new.

And then the movement paused and Rose was alone. Stranded like a starfish against a rock. Only it was not a rock, it was a display of makeup, skin care products, nail polish, and large blue bottles of nail polish remover.

Ha! she thought, seized one, and caught the next wave out.

At that moment, for the first time, the game changed. Perhaps because it was nail polish remover and Saffron had said, only an hour or two earlier, "I shall have to buy some more . . ."

Rose took it home, although she knew perfectly well she was stealing.

Nobody was watching, thought Rose.

Then, just as she was safely back home, passing under the fig tree, two steps from the door, she met David coming out.

She had forgotten all about him, and he startled her so much that she jumped and then said crossly, "I didn't know you were still here."

"I'm not really," said David, sounding, as he always seemed to sound, half a beat behind the rest of the world. "I've nearly gone."

Between David and the fig tree there was quite a large gap. It looked like there was plenty of room for

Rose to get by, if she had not minded stepping quite close to David. But she did mind, and so she stayed where she was.

David didn't seem to know he was in the way. He said, "We thought you must have gone swimming with Saffron and Sarah."

"Who did?"

"Me and Indigo."

There was an enormous animal solidity about David; he looked unshoveable, like a walrus on a beach. Also, he seemed to have forgotten he had been going anywhere. Rose thought (not for the first time) how unlike Tom he was. Tom would have said, "Hi, Permanent Rose! Thought you'd gone forever!" and vanished before Rose could say, "Stay."

David showed no signs of vanishing. If anything, he seemed to be swelling even larger. He said, "Where've you been?"

"Nowhere," said Rose, fidgeting from one foot to another.

David looked at her more carefully. Clearly she had come from town. And what was she carrying? A bottle of nail stuff. Price still on it. No bag. David had done a bit of shoplifting in his time, and he knew the signs all too well. He said, "You're going to get caught, you know!"

Instinctively Rose's hands clutched her bottle. "How d-do you . . . ?" she asked, stammering a little, and then began again. "You don't know what I've been doing!"

"I do." David glanced down at the bottle of nail polish remover and then up again to watch as Rose's pale face slowly bloomed redder and redder.

"Taking stuff," said David.

Rose had recently taken to wishing people were dead. At that moment the longing for David to be dead was so intense it made her dizzy. However, it had no effect at all on David. He remained inconveniently alive.

But he did not move. Not until they heard the sound of voices coming along the road, Saffron and Sarah back from their swim. At the sound of those laughing voices a look of terror swept over David's face, and all at once he jerked into action and began a blundering run that propelled him first into Sarah's wheelchair and then onto Saffron's chest.

"Which one of us are you throwing yourself at?" inquired Saffron. "Or is it purely random? Oh, he's gone!"

"Couldn't face seeing you with your clothes on!" said Sarah. "Flattering or insulting? Probably which?"

Rose did not wait to hear any reply. She felt far from up to spending time with Saffron and Sarah. She escaped into the house and headed for Indigo's room. All the Cassons were quite good at putting up with each other, but Indigo was the best at putting up with Rose.

Right now Rose felt like someone to put up with her was what she needed most of all.

Indigo's room was the tidiest in the house. It was also the smallest, just space enough for a bed, a chair (draped in clothes), and a huge wardrobe that contained everything he owned and quite a lot of things owned by other people too. Tom's old guitar lay on the bed. He had left it behind for Indigo when he went home to America. Rose picked it up and asked, "Can I play it?"

"Help yourself," said Indigo, and went back to the book he had been trying to read all afternoon.

Rose picked at the strings, the way she had seen Tom and Indigo do, but it did not sound like either of them were playing. She strummed hard over the sound hole, but that sounded worse. She changed her fingers in random patterns on the fingerboard. The bass strings buzzed horribly.

"Want me to show you how to do it properly?" asked Indigo when the sound became completely unbearable.

"No."

"Okay."

Rose put the guitar down and began to fiddle with Indigo's postcards. He had hundreds of them, old and new, photographs and paintings, ads and jokes, not lined up in rows but tacked up all over the walls. Rose fiddled down three Harley-Davidson motorbikes, a view of Earth from space, instructions for what to do in the event of abduction by aliens, and an advertisement for cocoa. Then she stuck them back up in the wrong places.

Indigo gave a big sigh and put down his book and asked, "What's the matter then, Rose?"

"Nothing."

"What's that you've got?"

"Nail polish remover for Saffy. Because she used up all hers getting my tattoos off."

"Good old Saffy," said Indigo, and he took the bottle, looked at it critically, unscrewed the lid, sniffed, remarked, "Not very nice," and gave it back to her.

Rose sighed with relief. She had shown it to him as a sort of test, half expecting him to say, "How did you pay for that? Where did you get it from? Shoplifting?"

But there had been no need for her to worry. In the Casson family, money was kept in a jam jar labeled HOUSEKEEPING on the kitchen mantelpiece. Anyone in the family was free to help themselves, anytime they liked. So there was no reason that Indigo should say, "How did you pay for that?" And even if the housekeeping jar had been empty he would not have thought of asking, "Shoplifting?" Nor would any of the family. They generally dealt with the ever-recurring problem of the empty jar by shaking it and staring hopefully at its grimy bottom, waiting for a miracle.

Now that Rose had passed the test, she looked at the bottle of nail polish remover with a sort of affectionate pride. She unscrewed the top and splashed some on for perfume because she liked the smell. Then she put the top back and shook it very hard to see if it would bubble. After that she wet her finger with a drop and tried squeaking it on the window. Indigo moved the guitar out of the reach of damage and picked up his book again.

"Read a bit to me," said Rose.

Indigo obligingly read:

> **And then Sir Lancelot knocked at the gate with the pommel of his sword, and with that came his host, and in they entered Sir Kay and he.**

Rose had read one book in her life, and when she had finished it (dragged through it by her father in an effort to educate her), she had read no more. And in her opinion books were for those unable to entertain themselves in any other way. For those who could not draw, who had no ears, who had no one to whom they might speak, who could not switch on a television or walk out of a room or stare out of a window or daydream or suck their knees, these people, she thought, might possibly be able to find a use for a book. Someone stuck in an empty concrete cell with nothing they could use to write on the walls might be grateful for a book, admitted Rose, although even then if they had any imagination, they would use the pages to manufacture paper boats and planes. Therefore, she had not hoped for much in the way of entertainment when she asked Indigo to read a bit, but even so, she had not expected quite such utter rubbish.

She said, "That sounds so stupid! How are you supposed to know what a pommel is? It's not even written properly!"

"That's just what David said," said Indigo.

"You read it to David?"

"Yep. And he said just the same as you. He thought it sounded stupid too."

Rose thought she had better give Indigo's book another chance.

"Read a bit more."

"All right," said Indigo. "Who does this remind you of?"

'Sir,' said his host, 'I weened ye had been in your bed.'

'So I was,' said Sir Lancelot, 'but I arose and leapt out at my window for to help an old fellow of mine.'

"Do you remember how Tom used to get out of his bedroom window?"

"To play his guitar on the roof," said Rose.

"That's right. It made me think of him straight away. It's not really stupid, this book. It's just old. It's got nice words in it. I keep finding more and more."

Indigo turned some pages and read,

> **Then the king looked about the world, and saw afore him in a great water a little ship, all apparelled with silk down to the water, and the ship came right unto them and landed on the sands.**

For a moment Rose saw in her mind a little ship with shining sails moving across an evening sea, but she asked, "Who was Sir Lancelot?"

Chapter Three

INDIGO HAD DISCOVERED LANCELOT MORE THAN FIVE WEEKS before, the night that Tom flew back to America.

A book had fallen onto his head.

This was not particularly surprising: Eve's housekeeping arrangements meant that things fell on people's heads quite often. Earlier that particular day, in a burst of Bill-inspired tidying, Eve had stacked a pile of books on top of Indigo's wardrobe. She had done it rather haphazardly because she was crying a bit at the time, still being very fond of Bill and not as cheerful about being dumped for Samantha as she pretended to the children. It was a very wobbly stack of books that Eve made through her tears.

In the night the top layer had fallen down.

The one that hit Indigo was a thick, shabby paperback with a broken orange spine. It had fallen open, and a sentence or two had caught his eye, the part where Lancelot jumped out of his bedroom window, the same little bit that he had just read to Rose.

When Indigo read those lines, Tom did not feel a thousand miles away, speeding through the darkness to a country Indigo had never seen. Instead he suddenly seemed quite close. No one would have been more likely than Tom to leap from his window to help a friend in trouble.

Indigo could not sleep the night that Tom went. The book had been company, its archaic language a code to crack, its green and ancient landscape a place where he would rather be, and its characters surprisingly familiar.

"Who *was* Sir Lancelot?" asked Rose again.

"He was the one they all liked best," said Indigo. "He was the one they all wanted to stay a bit longer. Lancelot did the bravest things (and the daftest things too). He had loads of friends, but a lot of the time he just went off on his own."

"Why did he jump out of the window?"

"Because three madmen had just chased his friend Kay through the forest and were about to slay him. He didn't actually jump though! He used his sheet to slide."

"How d'you know?"

"It says."

"So then did Kay and him fight the other three?"

"No. Lancelot fought them on his own."

"All three together?"

"Yep."

"Then what?"

"Lancelot won. And then he and Kay went back into the castle together and had another supper. And after that they went to bed, and in the morning Lancelot got up very early, took Kay's armor and his shield and his horse, and rode away with them while Kay was still asleep."

"Why?"

"Joke."

"Did Lancelot always win?"

"Not always."

"Let me look."

There was quite a lot in *Le Morte D'Arthur* that Indigo had no intention of sharing with Rose, but nevertheless he passed the book over with no hesitation at all. He guessed he would be quite safe.

Rose was a terrible reader. The sight of printed words gave her exactly the same queasy feeling that looking down from a height gave to Indigo, and butchers' shops gave to Eve. All the same she looked down hopefully, just in case this book should happen to be different from all the others she had encountered.

But it wasn't. It was hideous. It was the worst yet.

The cheap paper was soft with age, and was a stale yellowish color that reminded Rose of cheese. The print was gray and packed. There were no pictures. She turned a page and came across a block of italics blindly groping across the paper.

Yuck, thought Rose, looking quickly away. She did not say it, though, because she didn't want Indigo remarking, "Exactly what David said!" Instead she made herself look again.

It was no good. No little ship came sailing out of the water toward her. No reckless knight leaped from a window to help a friend in the night. And all the bright riders and comrades and lovers, all the shadowy forests with their wells and glades and apple trees, were hidden from Rose. The murky gray paragraphs of print concealed them completely.

"I can see it's written in English," she said at last. "But I can't read it. I can't make the words stick together to show me anything. They go all muddled and blurry, like a dream."

"It *is* muddled and blurry," agreed Indigo. "It's like a dirty, blurry window. But behind all the blur is another world I never knew about. And every time I get a new bit to make sense it's like I've cleared another little patch of window and I can see a bit farther."

Indigo picked up his guitar and began trickling up and down the notes of a chord.

"What do you see through the window?"

"People."

"Magic people?"

"Mmmm?" asked Indigo, head bent, listening to his guitar.

"Were they magic people? Lancelot and Kay and the others?"

"No, no." Indigo paused his playing to fiddle with the tuning pegs. "This guitar slips out of tune all the time. Listen! That better?"

"I don't know."

"They weren't magic people," said Indigo, trickling worse than ever now. "Their world was strange, all forests and lakes and enchanted castles . . . Actually, it was probably no weirder really than this one, I don't suppose. . . ."

Is this one weird? wondered Rose. Yes, it is.

"But Lancelot and Kay and all the others . . . ," continued Indigo, carefully strumming his chord. "Lancelot and Kay and the rest, they were just like us."

Rose waited. No more information came. Indigo forgot she was there and became absorbed in breaking down and building up another chord. He did not mean to get rid of Rose, but all the same it did get rid of Rose.

Caddy had heard of Indigo's people. She was back from the pub now, cleaning out the guinea pigs' cages in a bikini that Saffron had discarded as too obvious, yellow rubber gloves, and Wellington boots. She was her usual cheerful self again and said she had once read a book about Sir Lancelot that was far too complicated to explain to Rose.

"He went on quests," she said. "They all did. Questing all the time."

"What are quests?"

"Dares. Or big searches for stuff. Right now I'm questing for my old address book. Tell me if you see it, Rosy Pose!"

"What, in there?" asked Rose, looking in disgust at the stuff Caddy was shoveling into a bucket.

"No, of course not in here!" said Caddy, laughing, "And don't pull faces like that! It's only poo! You have to get used to poo! Even gorgeous Lancelot pooed!"

"No he didn't!"

"Of course he did. . . . Gallop through the forest . . . stop for a poo . . . bash off someone's helm, rescue a maiden . . . stop for a poo. . . . Everyone does it. Unless they're dead."

"Well, he's dead!" said Rose, triumphantly producing the only fact she knew for sure about Sir Lancelot. "So! Anyway, why do you want your old address book?"

"Just to look at."

"Why did they go questing? What did they do it for?"

"Love, nearly all the time," said Caddy, falling out of Saffron's bikini and stuffing herself back in again with guinea-piggy hands. "Love, the poor dopes!"

"Oh," said Rose, but when Caddy was safely busy with her head stuck inside the hutch scraping away at the corners with a trowel, she asked very thoughtfully, "Dopes?"

"What?" asked Caddy, backing out. "Oh, Rose! Are you still there? What did you say?"

"I was talking to myself."

"Sorry! Well, since you *are* still here, would you like to empty that bucket into a garbage bag for me, Rosy Pose?"

"No, thank you."

"Could you just hold the bag then, while I do it?"

"No. In case it gets on me."

"It won't."

"Or in case I have to breathe near it."

"Hold your breath."

"I don't like looking at it either."

"Rose!"

"Actually, I'm *not* still here," said Rose, and she disappeared very quickly indoors. There she found Saffron and Sarah searching for food in the kitchen because swimming had made them terribly hungry. Rose came in just in time to hear Sarah ask plaintively, "Why ask someone over for supper if there isn't any supper? What if my mum is making something fantastic and I am missing it for nothing?"

"Go home then," said Saffron, as she turned through the pages of the only cookbook Eve possessed (Christmas present from Bill at least four years before and still immaculate). "Go home if you like. Or hunt through the fridge and stop moaning! No one's ever starved here yet!"

"No, but there always has to be a first time," said Sarah as she pulled open the fridge door. "And think how upset you would be if it was me! (I leave you everything, by the way: the entire contents of my bedroom; how inconvenient is that?) There's practically nothing in this fridge but Diet Coke! Diet Coke and tubes of paint! Why would Eve keep paint in the fridge?"

"Why would anyone?" asked Saffron. "Hello, Rosy Pose! Didn't see you there! You're an artist. You will know. Why would Eve keep paint in the fridge?"

"It's handy there, isn't it?" asked Rose, surprised at such a silly question, and they were still laughing when Caddy and Eve came in.

Eve Casson was a garden-shed artist. She painted pictures in the garden shed, which was her favorite place in the world and contained all the luxuries she could imagine desiring: a shabby pink sofa to sleep on, a kettle to make black coffee (instant), and unlimited peace. When she wasn't in the shed painting pictures of anything that anyone would buy ("Not exactly Art" was how Bill described Eve's pictures), she was teaching at the college, or giving lessons in old people's homes, or helping young offenders turn into young artists instead. This summer, however, with the college closed until autumn, and the young offenders and old ladies too hot to feel like painting, she had found a new job: decorating the long gray walls and waiting rooms of the local hospital with inspiring and cheering art.

"I hate it, I hate it, I hate it!" she moaned, flopping down in a kitchen chair, all sandals and painty cheesecloth. "I'm sure I'll catch something dreadful! Do I smell? I feel like I smell. I wish I'd never said I'd do it! I'd have chucked it weeks ago, but they're all so grateful! Pass me a drink, Sarah darling, since you are so close to the fridge!"

Sarah passed her a Diet Coke, and Eve took a few huge gulps, topped up the can with gin from a bottle on the windowsill, and felt better.

"I've been painting copies of Greek statues all over Geriatrics," she told them. "Cheered them up no end, all the old men saying, 'I used to look like that!' and all the old ladies saying, 'Shocking! Oh, they are lovely!' Promise you'll shoot me, Saffy darling, before I get that old!"

"I promise," said Saffron.

"Rose will help you," said Eve, taking another swig from her can. "Have you had a good day, Rosy Pose? What made you decide to clean off your tattoos?"

"They were admired by that awful boy Indigo knows," said Caddy (who had taken off her boots and yellow gloves but was still having problems with the bikini). "That fat one who always smells of sweets . . ."

"I know. PatrickJoshMarcus," said Eve, pouring a little more gin into her Coke.

"David," said Saffron, and then she and Rose described David's arrival in the garden (with embellishments) to Caddy and Eve.

Eve suggested very solemnly that perhaps in the future Saffron might warn people when naked sunbathing was going on in the garden.

"How, exactly?" inquired Sarah, and Eve said maybe a little notice on the gate.

"They would have half the town coming to visit," observed Caddy.

"Darling, do you think so?" asked Eve. "Yes, you are probably right, if my geriatrics are anything to go by!

What are you doing with that horrible book, Saffy? Surely it's too hot to be hungry . . ."

"We're starving to death," said Saffron.

"Ring for pizza," said Eve.

"What, again?"

"We can have a lovely picnic in the garden," said Eve, but it did not turn out to be very lovely. Rose discovered that every pizza had been contaminated with olives and refused to eat any of them. Tom's name was accidentally mentioned, and Saffron and Sarah began a two-part lament on the subject of how Indigo could have let Tom go back to America without thinking to get his telephone number or address or any other means of communicating with him. Indigo (who had been hearing this all summer) got cross, put on his earphones, turned up the sound on his CD player so loud everyone could hear the buzz, and refused to communicate. Eve grew tearful and said, "Poor Tom! I blame myself. I should have asked. I am totally inefficient. No wonder Bill feels he needs a break (poor darling) . . ."

"A break?" asked Saffron. "What a cheek! His life is one long break!"

"A break from me, I meant. . . ." (Eve blew her

nose on a napkin, didn't know what to do with the napkin, sat on it, looked pleased at solving a problem, and cheered up.) "You mustn't be cross with him, Saffy! He is still your father as much as ever."

"No, he isn't," said Saffron.

"Saffy darling!" said Eve.

"Bill isn't *my* father," stated Saffron so loudly that even Indigo heard. "And I have been thinking that I should like to know who is."

All Saffron's family stared at her as if she had suddenly grown horns. Even Rose (who had been eating tomato sauce sandwiches behind a guinea-pig hutch in a martyred sort of way) crawled out for a proper look.

"Bill will be back, Saffy darling," said Eve, patting her hand. "This Samantha thing will pass . . ."

Then there was the most tremendous argument about whether the Samantha thing could possibly pass, and what that had to do with Saffy's father (Nothing, said Saffy), and while they were arguing they covered a lot of other topics as well, such as whether Indigo's hearing would be damaged by too much music played too loudly in times of stress, and how Rose was allowed to do exactly as she liked, and whether or not Caddy's lovely Michael should expect her to marry him on the strength of one diamond, ninety-seven driving lessons, a postcard from Spain, and several bunches of flowers nicked from the flower beds in the local park, and they probably would have gone on for very much longer if Rose had not suddenly toppled over on the grass.

Fast asleep.

Chapter Four

ALL SUMMER LONG INDIGO HAD BEEN SAYING HOW RIDICULOUS it was for anyone to expect a letter from Tom.

"He is not the letter-writing sort," he told Rose. "He never wrote a letter to America all the time he was here. Not once! He told me that himself. And he was here for months! Maybe he doesn't even know how to *send* a letter."

"He knows how to write," said Rose, who had once received a note from Tom. "So."

She was a very stubborn person. Every morning she got up early and hung around the street by the front door, hoping.

Even when the postman had passed (always without a glance her way), she still waited, just in case he found he had missed a letter and he turned back. But he never did.

• • •

That last Tuesday of summer, Rose was loitering in the early morning sunlight when Caddy's Michael came along in his driving instructor's car. He pulled up a little way before the Casson house, climbed out, and crossed to a nearby garden where he stood, chin in hand, studying with narrowed eyes the roses tangling over the fence. Then he made his decision and reached down. A moment later he was back in his car and driving very slowly along to Rose, steering with his knees while he carefully de-thorned the flower he had just stolen.

Today it was a pink one.

Rose had had a rose every morning ever since Michael first noticed her watching for the postman. They had come from gardens all over town. Michael said he was the Early Morning Rose Delivery Service, bringing roses to Roses. So she never had to go in from her postman-loitering empty-handed; she could always go in sniffing a rose.

"Going to be another hot one," remarked Michael, as he handed Rose her rose.

"What is?"

"The day. So I'm coming around about four-ish for iced tea."

"Iced tea?"

"With lots of lemon, please. That all right?"

"Wouldn't you rather have wine?" asked Rose, thinking of Bill. "Or diet Coke with gin in it like Mummy?"

"No, thank you, Rose," said Michael, laughing. "I'll see you later then? Four o'clock. No problem?"

"No problem," said Rose. She and Michael were very good friends. It was Rose who had gone with him to choose Caddy's engagement ring. If Michael wanted lemon tea at four o'clock that afternoon, then as far as Rose was concerned, he should have it. Even though until that morning she had never heard of such a thing, couldn't imagine how it was made, and had a vision of lots of lemons in a teapot, which she was sure could not be right.

"Good," said Michael, and started up his engine as if he were going to drive away, and then seemed to change his mind and turned it off again.

"Rosy Pose?" he asked.

"Mmmm?"

"I've been thinking. I'm not going to get that ring we chose handed back to me, am I?"

"Oh, Michael!"

"Just a thought."

"Would you be very sad if it were?" asked Rose fearfully.

"Well," said Michael, "I think it would be fair enough to say I would be a bit sad, yes."

"What would you do?"

"Take myself away, I suppose."

Rose nodded. She supposed he would.

"I notice you did not immediately say, 'Michael, I am sure Caddy would never think of such an awful thing!'"

"I am *sure* Caddy would not think of such an awful thing!" said Rose at once, but she said it with her eyes shut and her fingers crossed behind her back.

Michael noticed this, but he did not ask any more questions. He just smiled and said, "Thanks, Rosy Pose. You can open your eyes now." And then he drove away.

Rose sat on the doorstep and she sniffed her rose,

and she thought about how bad it would be if Caddy gave her diamond ring back to Michael, causing Michael (a bit sadly) to take himself away. Rose had completely and utterly had enough of people taking themselves away that summer. She thought and thought, and after a while she thought of a way to prevent it.

Caddy could not give back a ring she did not have.

This solution was so simple she was surprised it had not occurred to her at once. Tom would have thought of it, she was sure. Sir Lancelot would have considered it the obvious thing to do. Now Rose (successful shoplifter and student of archaic chivalry) thought of it too.

Luck was with her. When she returned to the house, Caddy was out of bed and splashing about in the bathroom. Rose searched through Caddy's bedroom with the ferocious intensity of a dozen burglars, she found Caddy's diamond ring in its little blue box, and she took it out of the box and she stole it.

"I am not really stealing it," said Rose to Rose, as she pushed it into her pocket. "I am taking it to keep it safe."

It sounded good, but it did not feel good. Rose did

not need anyone to tell her that if she took someone's diamond ring without telling them, it was stealing.

"*Good* stealing," said Rose to comfort herself. "Like Michael getting my roses. Is that bad stealing? No! This is just the same."

That felt much better.

"Anyway, it's for a very good cause," said Rose to Rose.

Caddy's ring had come from a jeweler who made his own designs. This was because Rose and Michael, after searching the usual shops armed with Michael's credit card and Rose's enormous ability to spend other people's money, had decided that nothing in any of them was good enough for Caddy.

"When I buy diamonds for myself," Rose had said at one point, "they will be quite big, and they will be in silver rings. Not gold. They will look much starrier in silver."

That was why Caddy's ring was a quite-big diamond in platinum, not gold. It looked like a star in a knot of light.

It burned in the pocket of Rose's chopped-off jeans. It felt as if she had stolen a flame. She could not stop checking in the mirror to see if the light was shining through.

"You look perfect, darling," said Eve, noticing Rose inspecting her reflection for the third time that morning.

"Oh, good," said Rose. "Do you know how to make iced tea?"

"No," said Eve, who did not know how to make anything much. "I can't even imagine! It's probably one of those things that ordinary people can't do because you need so much equipment. Like cappuccino coffee. And popcorn."

Rose said that Sarah's mother had a cappuccino coffee machine, and a popcorn maker too, but added fairly that she was far too rich to be considered an ordinary person.

"She can't help being rich," said Eve kindly, stirring instant coffee into diet Coke, a potion she called Brain Juice, and would never let Rose try. "Want to come to the hospital this morning and help me paint pictures on the walls?"

"No, thank you," said Rose, fiddling with the ring in her pocket.

"You haven't forgotten what we said about not going into town on your own?"

One of the things that had emerged during the huge noisy conversation the night before was the fact that (not for the first time) Rose had wandered off into town all by herself. And all of Rose's family except Rose agreed that nine years old was much too young for such behavior.

("But I am not nine!" Rose had protested, and very nearly fooled them. Until they remembered she was eight.)

"Rosy Pose?" repeated Eve, who was waking up a bit more now. "About going into town? You haven't forgotten?"

Rose did not say whether she had forgotten or not, but she suddenly noticed how tired Eve was looking and hugged her, although she was not generally a great hugger.

"Are you sad because Saffy wants to know who her father was?" Rose asked.

Eve paused for a moment, and then she sighed and said, "I suppose I always guessed she would."

"Do you know?"

"Linda never told me. She was in Italy, and I was in England. Too far away. She never said a word until Saffy was born."

"But she was your sister!"

"I know. And we always shared everything when we were growing up. But it was different when she went away."

"Did you quarrel?"

"No, no, no! I missed her very much. I still do. I always will. But you don't know how difficult it is, Rose, to stay a part of someone's life when they are suddenly far away."

"Yes, I do!" said Rose at once. "Daddy went away. And Caddy goes off for weeks and weeks to college. And now Tom."

"I suppose you do know then," agreed Eve. "So you can understand how it was for Linda and me. Now, then! Hospital! I've finished my rude nudes for the oldies, thank goodness! Back to the children's ward today! Much more cheerful! I keep thinking of new pictures for them. What are you going to do with yourself, Rose?"

"Can I draw on the wall by the stairs?"

Eve said of course she could, gave her a handful of crayons and charcoal to experiment with, kissed the top of her head, and left for the hospital. Rose sat on the bottom stair and on the wall beside drew a little ship sailing through a starry night toward a beach. She used a blue crayon for the ship, and the charcoal for the silky shadows on the sails and the silky ripples on the sea. Then she hitched herself up a stair higher, found a red crayon instead of blue, and began to draw Lancelot getting out of his window.

Rose was the real artist of the Casson family. More than Eve, who really preferred sleeping to art. More than Bill, who had his own studio in London, exhibitions in all sorts of expensive and exclusive places, and his own Web site where anyone who wanted could admire samples of his art and read for free his modest remarks on inspiration, respect, and the importance of not being swept away by public acclaim.

Rose drew and painted the way other people daydream. She did not need an audience, and she did not care very much what anyone thought. She was very much in everyone's way while drawing on the stairs, but her family all stepped around her without too much fuss. They knew she did not like drawing on paper.

The stairs were a very good place for waylaying people. Rose waylaid Saffron, who told her how to make iced tea, a skill that she had learned from

Sarah's mother, and supervised while Rose did it in an ordinary glass jug with no special equipment at all.

"You have to remember to take the tea bags out," Saffy told her. "And you need to put in a tiny bit of sugar or else it tastes of leather. And it's better with lemons. Then you just put it in the fridge until it's really cold. That's it! You can go back to your stair! Want to come to Sarah's with me for lunch? Sarah's mother said we could."

"Yes, please, but not now."

"Later, then."

Caddy was the next person to be stopped by Rose. She fell right over her, which she admitted at once was her own fault for not looking where she was going. Caddy had found her old address book and was looking up past boyfriends.

"They must have been okay," she said, rubbing her shins and sitting down to chat. "Or else why would I have kept their names? But I can't seem to remember so many of them! Who on earth was J. Hamster?"

"He was ages ago," said Rose at once. "His name was Jeff and he gave you a hamster. So Indy and Saffron and me used to call him J. Hamster. Don't you remember?"

"I do now! Oh well. I'll cross him out then. I don't want any more hamsters! Patrick?"

"He was the one who never knew which day it was. And you were always calling him Peter by mistake. Peter was the one who patted Indigo's bum . . ."

"And mine," called Saffron from the kitchen.

"I do remember Peter," said Caddy, scribbling vigorously. "He was a big mistake! Alex, anyone?"

No one could remember Alex. Caddy scribbled again and continued, "Jonathan, turned into an accountant. Derek, gave him to Mum and she dumped him. . . . Sean . . . Oh, this is so depressing! I'm sure I never knew a Sean!"

"I wonder," remarked Saffron, coming to join them on the stairs, "if my mother forgot who my father was. Or if he was just someone who passed anonymously by in the night. Like all these boyfriends of yours seem to have done!"

"They didn't pass anonymously," said Caddy indignantly. "I wrote them down!"

Rose, listening thoughtfully, was feeling better and better about taking Caddy's ring. She thought if Lancelot could steal a horse for a joke, then without question she could steal a diamond to help out a friend in need. It would be dreadful if Michael should become just another crossed-out name in Caddy's address book. She asked, "Is Michael written down in there, Caddy?"

Caddy said a little defensively that of course he wasn't, as if she would need to write down Michael! She only wrote down the ones she might possibly forget.

"But you have forgotten half of them," pointed out Saffron and Rose at once.

Caddy said, "Well then, that just proves . . ." and before they could argue anymore, she announced that she was going shopping for Eve and would buy anything they asked for.

"Lemons," said Rose at once.

"Lemons," said Caddy and went, leaving Rose with Saffy and Indigo to look after her. A little later on Saffron went off to Sarah's, so that left just Indigo and Rose.

Indigo had been reading *Le Morte D'Arthur* again. He sat down with it in his hand a stair or two above Rose, admired her red and blue pictures, and said, "I've found someone else you will like. Percival who got lost in the wilderness visiting his aunt. He made friends with a lion . . . Here they are! You read it! Look, Percival goes up to a rock . . ."

Following Indigo's finger Rose read, "'. . . and found the lion which always kept him . . .'"

"'Fellowship,'" said Indigo. "Go on!"

"'. . . and he stroked him upon the back . . .' Caddy said they were dopes, Lancelot and Kay and all them."

"I quite like dopes," said Indigo. "What's that disgusting slime in the saucer?"

"Egg white. Raw. To help glue the charcoal on. They used it in the olden days to stick the paint to the walls. Sarah told me about it. Have you got any more Lancelot bits I could draw?"

"There's one here. It's a chapter heading. It says, 'How Sir Lancelot rode on his adventure, and how he helped a dolorous lady from her pain . . .'"

"What's *dolorous* mean?" interrupted Rose, using her fingers to smudge dark shadows under forest trees.

"Moaning and groaning. Don't suck your fingers, Rose, that's disgusting! This girl was stuck by magic in a bath of boiling water for five years, until Lancelot came along and fished her out . . ."

"Did she have any clothes on?"

"What, in the bath? Of course not. She was . . ." Indigo paused to find the place in the book. "She was 'naked as a needle!'"

"'Naked as a needle'?" Rose repeated, smiling because the words gave her such a vision of sharp, shining brightness.

"Lucky it was Lancelot who came along then! Not someone like David! David wouldn't have fished her out. He'd have just stared and stared!"

"You never give David a chance!"

Rose looked cross and did not reply. She really could not understand Indigo's willingness to forgive David. She herself would happily have detested him forever and ever and ever.

"So anyway," continued Indigo cheerfully. "Everyone was very pleased with Lancelot, and they said that since he'd got the girl out of the bath with no bother, he might as well kill the dragon that was hanging around too."

Rose had always liked dragons. They were her sort of animal. She had never cared much for the family guinea pigs and hamsters.

"Were there truly dragons in those days?" she asked, forgetting to be cross.

"Yes, and dwarves and lions and serpents and enchanters, and a hundred miles of forest in every direction . . . There will be again one day, when all the people go. . . . It will all come back. Anyway, this dragon: it says,

> **A horrible and fiendly dragon, spitting fire out of his mouth.**
>
> **Then Sir Lancelot drew his sword and fought with the dragon long, and at last with great pain Sir Lancelot slew the dragon.**

"What happens to dragons when they get slain?" asked Rose.

"Oh," said Indigo. "They turn into comets. And sail among the planets on the trade winds of the stars."

"Always?"

"Yep. Every single time."

The Lancelot in Rose's picture looked just like Tom. Same dark hair and eyes. Same amused, couldn't-care-less expression. Same scuffed up sneakers and black denim jacket.

Rose added a sign above his head. NEW YORK.

After she had finished, she sat thinking for a long time. She made no attempt to begin with drawing the dragon or the girl in the bath. She did not seem to notice when Indigo took his book back upstairs again, but when he climbed back over her, coming down, she said, "We should go back to his house. Where Tom stayed with his grandmother."

"I told you, Rose, I've been. It's all shut up. His grandmother must have gone over to America too."

"She might be back now."

"Don't think so, Rosy Pose. Here's Caddy home again! Coming to help unload?"

"All right," agreed Rose, and left her drawing to help heave shopping from the back of Caddy's dilapidated car.

"Lemons," said Caddy, handing her a couple when they were back in the kitchen.

"Thank you," said Rose, and after a little puzzled thought she dropped both of them whole into her jug of lemon tea. After that she went back and looked at Lancelot on the stairs for a while and then called to Caddy and Indigo in the kitchen, "I'm going to Sarah's for lunch. Saffy's there. She said I could."

"Okay," replied Caddy peacefully. No one had ever

objected to Rose going to Sarah's house alone. It was only a three-minute walk up the street from their own home.

It was not a three-minute walk by the route that Rose took. Rose's way took her halfway across town, to the house where, when Tom was in England, he had lived with his grandmother.

By now the morning was bright with heat. Rose, who saw the world in terms of pictures, thought that if she had wanted to paint it, she would need the sort of colors they were expected to use at school. Flat yellows and oranges and hopeless, unshining greens. She squinted up at the sun as if to ask what it was thinking of to allow such unpleasantness. The sun glared back down at her like an overbearing adult who had finished with pandering to the likes of Rose.

She began to feel very little.

Arriving at Tom's old home made her feel even smaller, but that was because of the trees.

They were huge dark yews, growing all around the garden and on both sides of the drive that led from the road to the shabby old house. The blinding sunlight cut black shadows across the grass, but it could not penetrate the darkness under those trees. Beneath them the air seemed heavy and very still. As if no one had moved through it for a long, long time.

All the same, Rose hardly hesitated before she plunged in. Somewhere, she hoped, there would be a clue as to where Tom had gone. A message that would make a link. In Rose's world people left messages for each other when they went away. Eve pinned pieces of paper on the door when she went out:

Key under that flat stone

or

Come in, darlings, back whenever

or

Sarah's lovely mum cooking tonight

Sarah's mother was also a great message leaver. Notes in milk bottles saying:

Semiskimmed only in future, as I have asked many times before

or

We will be away the following days. Please close the gate this time.

Even Bill left messages, Post-its on the fridge when he went back to London. There were several there right now:

ANY TIME, DARLINGS, ALWAYS
WITH LOVE,
DADDY

also

DARLING EVE,
REMEMBER THE GOOD TIMES

and

£250 IN HOUSEKEEPING JAR

HAVE THROWN AWAY BUTTER, YOGURTS AND CHEESE

ALL PAST SELL-BY DATES

ALSO SALAD

DO TRY TO KEEP TRACK

XXX—BILL, AS EVER

Those were the sort of things that Rose was thinking of as she tiptoed under the yew trees and along the dusty drive to the house. She told herself she was looking for an address, but really she was looking for proof. Proof that whoever had gone from here still cared about the life that they had left behind. Or even just proof that they had been here at all.

It was amazing how unlived-in a garden could grow in just over a month. Gazing around, Rose understood exactly what Indigo had meant when he said the wild forest of *Le Morte D'Arthur* would all come back one day. It had started here already.

The grass was as long as wild grass, and weeds had spread across the gravel of the drive. Litter had blown in from the street and not been picked up. Even the trees themselves seemed to have stooped a little lower. A cat lay motionless with heat under the far hedge.

"Puss," called Rose.

Her voice came out thin and high. The cat did not move. Nothing in the whole garden moved. It looked like a place that nobody cared about anymore.

Rose turned to the house. It had the same deserted look. There was a film of dust dimming the windows.

How strange, thought Rose, touching the dust. The windows at the Casson house were hardly ever cleaned, but she had never noticed them being dusty. She wondered if windows that nobody looked through gradually become dimmer and dimmer. She wondered how the dust knew nobody looked.

There was no message pinned on the front door, and no empty milk bottles to hold notes either. She looked up at the letter box, wishing she could peer through it to see if there had been any post, but it was an old-fashioned narrow one and anyway, too high for Rose to reach. Heavy curtains had been drawn across the windows.

The whole place was as shut up as anywhere could possibly be.

Still, Rose did not quite give up hope. She set off

around the side of the house to investigate the back.

There was nothing there, either, but the back door did have a small bottle-glass window. If Rose stood on tiptoe, she could just see through this window into the hall. There, at last, she saw something moving, a tiny red light flashing on and off. Rose knew that it was the telephone, and the light was flashing to show that people had called and left messages.

Indigo and me, thought Rose. And Mummy and Caddy and Saffron and Sarah. Michael too, and Sarah's mother.

After Tom had gone, Rose knew that they had all tried at one time or another.

Nearly all those messages are probably from us, thought Rose, peering through the little window.

And then, standing there, looking at the telephone light flashing in the empty house, the back of Rose's neck suddenly prickled with fright. Fear swept over her like a cold wave.

Somebody was there, she was certain. Somebody was watching her from behind.

She did not know why she was so sure of it, but she was.

Perhaps I heard a sound, she thought, listening intently.

There was no sound now.

It was a long time before Rose could summon the courage to turn away from the window. She did not like to take her eyes from the little red light. It was somehow like a tiny talisman, flashing its messages from home.

It will still be there, Rose told herself.

It will be right behind me, she thought, trying to be brave.

Still she did not turn and look.

Perhaps, she thought in sudden hope, *I heard the cat! Perhaps the cat is watching me!*

Cats do watch, thought Rose, and at last she faced around.

There was sunlight and a ragged garden and the noise of traffic on the road beyond the hot, dark trees. No cat. Nothing moved.

There was nobody there.

Chapter Five

WHILE CADDY WAS SHOPPING FOR LEMONS, AND INDIGO WAS reading *Le Morte D'Arthur* and Rose was sitting on the stairs drawing pictures of her dreams on the wall, Saffron was at Sarah's house. Sarah had a computer connected to the Internet, and she had suggested that this might be useful in the search for Saffy's father.

"People do use the Internet to find relations," she said, as she led Saffron up the stairs to her enormous bedroom. "Pity you can't use it to lose relations as well. I have far too many . . . Come in then, Saffy! Welcome to the shrine! Mind the icon! Oh, too late . . ."

The icon, a life-size cardboard cutout of Sarah's favorite pop star, fell on his face, revealing the price of his presence (£19.99) unromantically printed on the back of his head.

"I can't imagine what you see in him," remarked Saffron, lifting him to his feet again. "Just look at him! What a poser!"

"I know," agreed Sarah. "He's a fad. I'll grow out of him soon. Like all the others." She nodded toward an untidy stack of discarded cardboard heroes brooding disconsolately in a corner. "Mum (who is not very up on style) thought I should send them off for recycling. I had to explain to her that no Casson would ever dream of sending anything off for recycling! But she got it in the end. She said, 'So they have to stay here forever, gathering dust?' Clever old thing! Did you know dust is the new cool, Saffy?"

"I can't see any dust here," objected Saffron, who had long ago given up being impressed by Sarah's bedroom, which contained far more of everything than any one person could possibly need. "No dust at all. Just piles and piles of loot!"

"Well, there would be dust if it weren't for the cleaner," said Sarah. "Surely you can see that there is theoretical dust! And I can't help the loot. It's nearly all donated by relations, mostly due to my tragic need for a wheelchair . . ."

"If much more piles up, you will have a tragic need for a forklift truck and a warehouse," commented Saffron, prowling around to see what had been added since her last visit.

"Oh well," said Sarah. "It makes them feel better, buying it, so I let them. Subtly guiding their taste, of course . . . Come on, let's find your mysterious father! The blue computer's the one with the phone line; the other one's just for games. . . . It would help if you knew his name."

"That's what we're trying to find," Saffron pointed out, clearing an armload of baseball caps off the blue computer's desk and switching it on. "What do you want me to do with all these?"

"Nothing. Dump them somewhere."

Saffron piled them on Sarah's bed and then sat down at the blue computer and looked at it uncertainly, wondering what she might find.

"Perhaps he's somewhere looking for you," suggested Sarah encouragingly. "Some very rich Italian probably, since you were born there. Pity you don't look Italian, Saffy! But you look like Caddy and Eve. Were your mum and Eve identical twins?"

"Yes. No one can tell them apart in the old photos we have. Let's put in my mother's name, and Siena, because I was born there, and do a search on that."

They did, and to their horror found over five thousand Web sites containing those three words.

"Going to be a long morning," commented Sarah, starting on page one, and on page three she said, "I hope he's worth it." And on page seven she said, "Of course, if he is a very rich Italian, he might whisk you off to his palace in Venice and we'd never see you again . . ."

"You can come and stay," said Saffron kindly, and opened up a site on Venice to show Sarah where she would be coming to visit.

They both looked at it thoughtfully for a minute.

"Terribly wet," said Saffron at last. "In fact, flooded! A bit scary to have a flood victim for a father. Good job you can swim so well, Sarah!"

"Yes," agreed Sarah, and then asked, "Do you want to see something really scary?" and opened up a site where Mrs. Warbeck, Sarah's mother, beamed down from a corner of the screen, describing and commentating on pictures of radiant school interiors that faded in and out of view all around her as she spoke.

"It's her school's new Web site," explained Sarah. "It's just finished. Doesn't she look exactly like an angel describing heaven? (Don't forget she booted her own daughter out of that gorgeous place!)"

"You forced her," said Saffron. "You deliberately allowed yourself to be reluctantly booted!"

"You're right. I did. But did you ever see anyone look so pleased with themselves!"

"Yes, I have," said Saffron at once, grabbing the keyboard and beginning to type. "I found it at school last term: 'Bill Casson, Seriously Now.'"

"What?"

Saffron pointed to the screen, where on a black background with an invisible gold pen the words "Bill Casson, Seriously Now" were being slowly inscribed.

"Welcome," said Bill's voice from the screen (speaking casually-and-with-a-hint-of-laughter), "to 'Bill Casson, Seriously Now.'"

"I wonder how many times he practiced that!" said Saffron. "Do you think Samantha helped him?"

"I bet she did! Wicked old Bill! Why do we still like him?"

"Because he's so civilized it's hard to believe he is wicked," Saffron answered. "You know how he is! Always says the right thing, always wears the right clothes . . ."

"And he's kind," said Sarah, remembering her Ferrari magazines.

"Kind, and a bit thick," agreed Saffron, watching as the gold letters faded off the screen. "Thinks he's an artist, and so do lots of other people. . . . Here comes his photo! Just look at that smile!"

"It's the Casson smile," said Sarah. "You all do it. Like you don't want to smile, but you can't help it. Slow, and then suddenly there. And a little bit guilty. I call it the Casson smile. Devastating . . . Come on, then! Here's the menu: 'Reviews, Site Map, Gallery, News'! Which do we want?"

"Not the reviews," said Saffron. "I've seen them. They are full of stuff about emotional honesty and Scandinavian roots (which are the thing to have, as everyone knows). Open up 'News.' See what he's up to."

"News" was a list of exhibitions, past and future. London, Copenhagen, Stockholm ("He really is digging for his Scandinavian roots, isn't he!" commented Sarah. "Nearly North Pole!"), Munich, New York.

"No wonder he hardly ever gets home," said Saffron. "Now look in the gallery! There's a picture of a carton of milk and a hat, called *Darkness Returning* . . ."

At the same time as Saffron and Sarah were commenting rudely on their relations' Web sites (and Eve was making sketches of everyone's teddy bears in the hospital children's ward, and Bill was checking out hotels in New York, and Michael was wistfully admiring the enormous motorbike beside him at a red traffic light, and Caddy was hunting for her diamond ring, and Indigo was telephoning David and getting his mother instead, while all these people were doing all these things), Rose was standing, still with fear, on the back doorstep of an empty house.

She could see no one, and she could hear no one, but she was still afraid. She wished Sir Lancelot (or even better, Tom) would jump out of a window and save her from whatever it was hiding among the trees. But Lancelot didn't and neither did Tom, and nor did anyone else.

So Rose had to save herself, and she jumped from the step, swerved around the side of the house, skidded and went sprawling on slippery dried yew needles, sprang up again, made it to the gate, heard something fall: Caddy's ring, which had worked its way out of her pocket, grabbed it up (grazing her knuckles), clutched it tight, and didn't stop running until she reached Sarah's house and Sarah's mother, watering tubs of blue and white flowers on the front porch, cool and immaculate and organized.

"Rose!" exclaimed Sarah's mother when she saw her,

and put down her watering can and took her straight to the kitchen. There she bathed her bleeding knees and hands, fetched her orange juice and paper towels, and tactfully didn't notice that Rose was transferring something from hand to hand and trying not to cry.

"Whatever *happened*?" she asked at last.

"I fell over."

"Does anyone know you are here?"

"Caddy and Indigo do," said Rose, and was very thankful that this happened to be true. "I thought Saffy was here."

"She's upstairs with Sarah," said Sarah's mother, passing Rose the kitchen telephone. "Just give Caddy or Indigo a quick call to let them know we have you safe, and then you can go up to find them."

Sarah's mother was used to being obeyed, so Rose rang quite meekly and said, "Hullo, Indigo, I'm at Sarah's."

"I know you are," said Indigo on the other end of the line.

"He says he knows I am," related Rose to Sarah's mother.

"Does Caddy?" asked Sarah's mother.

"Sarah's mum says, 'Does Caddy?'" Rose told Indigo.

"You know she does!" said Indigo, sounding so surprised that Sarah's mother heard him too. She laughed and said, "All right, Rose! I'm sorry! I fuss too much. Sarah tells me so every day. Tell Indigo I fuss too much!"

Rose passed this message on, and then said good-bye very quickly and put the phone down. She had not lied to Indigo, or to Sarah's kind mother, but she felt like she had. She tried to give Sarah's mother something good, to make up for having deceived her.

"Do you know about Lancelot and the dragon and the lady who was in the bath for five years?"

"Oh, yes," said Sarah's mother packing up her first-aid box. "Lovely stories. Legends."

"Legends?"

"Like Santa Cl—" Sarah's mother suddenly stopped and looked at Rose, and Rose could see her wondering whether there still was a Santa Claus in Rose's world. "Well, not like Santa Claus . . . I didn't mean to say that. . . . Like . . . who brings you Easter eggs, Rose? The Easter bunny?"

Rose said she didn't think so, and Sarah's mother looked relieved and said, "Well, like that!" and shooed Rose out of the kitchen.

Rose plodded up the stairs very slowly so as not to crease the beautiful new Band-Aids on her knees, pushed open Sarah's door, walked into the cardboard film star, and said, "Hello! What are you laughing at?"

"Come and look!" said Sarah, and turned the computer screen so that Rose could see the extremely long list of people Bill felt must be thanked for encouragement and inspiration. Mozart and Michelangelo were listed (with dates), but Eve, Caddy, Saffron, Indigo, and Rose were all lumped together in one brief comment: "And, of course, my wonderful family."

"No mention at all of me!" said Sarah.

Joking about Bill ("We found him while we were looking for Saffy's father"), making sandwiches for lunch in the kitchen, hurrying home to give Michael his iced tea ("Some people slice the lemons; some don't," remarked Michael), explaining that Caddy had suddenly rushed off, no one knew where, or why ("If you say so, Rosy Pose," said Michael sadly), all these things pushed the frighteningness of the morning further and further back in Rose's mind.

By bedtime the memory was hardly scary at all. Hardly scary, but very puzzling. A lingering feeling of being watched from behind traced up and down Rose's spine like a finger.

Someone was there, she thought. *I am sure someone was there, but it could not have been anyone bad. Nobody shouted at me, or chased after me, or tried to stop me from getting away.*

In the middle of the night, tossing and turning, too hot to sleep, she thought, *Perhaps it was Tom.*

Rose sat up in bed to think about this idea properly.

Tom had not wanted to go home to America. Perhaps he had found a way to come back. Perhaps he did not telephone or write because he was already here. Secretly here. That would be so like Tom.

The more Rose thought about it, the more it seemed that this must be true, until in the end she got up and crept into Indigo's room and shook him awake.

"Indy!" she whispered.

"What? What?" groaned Indigo, flinging up his arms as if to defend himself, still three-quarters asleep.

"Wake up!"

"Oh, not now, Rose! Okay, okay, I am awake! You can stop banging me about! What is it?"

"Indy, do you think Tom is here all the time?"

"Have you been having weird dreams, Rose?"

"No. I've been thinking. What if Tom is back at his old house, living secretly? Do you think he could be? Will you come with me to look?"

"Don't be daft, Rose!"

"Is it daft?"

"You know it is. Listen," Indigo sat up and switched on his bedside light. "Think how Tom left. On the first flight they could get him. Rushing, because his sister was so ill and he might be too late . . ."

"He didn't care a bit about her until she got ill," interrupted Rose.

"I know," agreed Indigo. "He'd been horrible about her. And that made it ten times worse for him. And as well, he knew we knew."

"What does that matter?"

"I think maybe that's why we haven't heard from him. Maybe he wants to forget about all the stuff that happened when he was over here."

"We are the stuff that happened when he was over here!" said Rose indignantly. "He can't forget about us! And we can't forget about him. Forgetting is not that easy. So!"

"Well, he knows where we are. Anytime he likes he can get in touch. He knows we're still here."

Indigo switched off his bedside light as if that was the end of the discussion. Rose switched it on again.

"How does he know we are still here? He might think we want to forget about him. Like you think he might want to forget about us. He might be thinking, 'Maybe they don't want to find me.'"

"We *can't* find him!" said Indigo. "We don't know where to begin. We'll just have to wait."

"We've waited all summer. Nothing has happened. It's like a game. Someone is going to have to go first!"

"And do what?"

"Just say, 'It's okay.' Just say, 'I'm still here.'"

"Good old Permanent Rose," said Indigo. "Go back to bed now, though. Take this with you if you like. It'll send you to sleep!"

He pulled *Le Morte D'Arthur* out from under his pillow, handed it to her, and lay down and shut his eyes.

"Night, night," he said firmly.

Reluctantly Rose went back to her own bed and looked at the book. The cover picture showed Arthur marrying Guinevere. They both looked terribly worried, and so did the watching congregation. Peering closely, Rose noticed that Guinevere's crown was slipping over one ear and Arthur had forgotten to put on his shoes.

Lancelot was nowhere in sight. Rose decided he was probably outside with Percival and the lion. She imagined them together, sitting on the church steps, chatting like friends:

"Did you see their faces when you turned up with a lion?"

"Typical Arthur, forgetting his shoes!"

I will *read it,* decided Rose determinedly, and she opened the book and peered inside it like someone might peer into a dirty paper bag. The usual repulsive gray print leered up at her in the dim light.

"'Sir,'" she deciphered, with great difficulty, "'Sir'—she—said . . . 'I—am—aclean' . . . 'I—am—a—clean . . . mad' . . . 'A—clean—maddn' . . . Maddn! Maddn! What's a maddn?"

Rose climbed out of bed again.

"What's a maddn?"

"Gosh!" moaned Indigo, blinking in the sudden light. "Are you back? That's my foot you're sitting on!"

"Sorry."

"This had better be good, Rosy Pose."

"I only want to know what a maddn is.

It says 'Sir'—she—said—'I—am . . . a—a—clean—maddn . . .' You told me to read it!"

"Show me then," groaned Indigo, holding out his hand, and when Rose had pointed he took the book and read, "'Sir,' she said, 'I am a clean maiden!' Oh! Actually, Rose, I don't know if you should be reading this bit!"

"Why? Is it rude?" asked Rose hopefully.

"Well. Not sure, let me look! Oh. Luckily nothing happens this time! There's this knight fast asleep, who wakes up to find some girl has climbed into bed beside him."

"And then does she tell him she's a clean maiden?"

"Yep."

"That's a funny thing to say in the middle of the night!"

"Mmmm."

"Was he cross?"

"He was annoyed but polite," said Indigo. "And he said, 'Fair damsel, arise out of this bed or else I will!'"

"Read that again!"

"'Arise out of this bed or else I will!'"

"Me or her?"

"Both of you," said Indigo firmly.

Chapter Six

ON WEDNESDAY ROSE'S ROSE FROM THE EARLY MORNING Rose Delivery Service was small and red, with golden stamens.

"Stick it behind your ear," ordered Michael, "like this!" and he leaned over so that Rose could see that he, too, had a small red rose, fastened behind his left ear.

"Gorgeous, or what?" he asked.

Michael had smooth black hair, fastened in a ponytail with a red elastic band. He also had narrow dark eyes, a gold earring, and a faded red shirt.

"Did you pick that rose to match your shirt?" asked Rose.

"Rose. I did."

"It's just right."

Michael nodded.

"But you don't look a bit like a driving instructor."

"Good."

"Don't you like being a driving instructor?"

“No.”

“Why d’you do it, then?”

“For money. Why d’you do the things you do, Rose?”

Rose, watching the postman walk past the Casson house without stopping, did not reply.

“For love,” said Michael, answering himself.

At the beginning of the summer, Eve had asked Sarah, “What do children in the hospital want more than anything?”

Sarah was a good person to ask. When she was younger, she had been in and out of the hospital for weeks on end. She knew exactly what children in the hospital want.

“Home,” she said.

All summer Eve had been collecting pictures of home for the children’s ward. She had a big folder full of sketches of washing on lines, cats on sofas, and dogs in gardens. She had sketched cluttered bathrooms, coat hooks overflowing with coats, beds with the teddies still in them and beds that had fallen in heaps on the floor. Also, she drew brothers in old sneakers sprawled in front of TVs, sisters in baths with bubbles up to their necks, fathers shaving while eating toast, and mothers on the phone drinking coffee. The walls and corridors of the children's ward were now bright with copies of these pictures. Eve showed her collection to Sarah when she arrived after breakfast that Wednesday morning.

"They are perfect," said Sarah, turning the pictures one by one. "Exactly what I meant! Eve, Dad said to tell you that you are all invited to a barbecue tomorrow night. It's for Mum's birthday. And do you think I could borrow your kitchen this morning to make a birthday cake? I've brought all the stuff and Saffy said she'd help."

Eve said of course she could, and stayed at home a little longer to add another picture to her collection, a kitchen table with a birthday cake being constructed upon it. Eve drew, Rose ate cherries soaked in brandy, and Saffron and Sarah broke eggs, melted chocolate and golden syrup into a dark and sticky goo, scattered flour everywhere, and reported the progress they had made in finding Saffron's father.

"We're more or less positive he's a very rich Italian living in Venice with no one to spend his money on," said Sarah, whisking egg whites so vigorously they flew into the air. "Does that sound possible, Eve?"

Eve said cheerfully that it sounded more than possible. In fact, exactly the sort of man her darling sister Linda would have been least able to resist. "And neither would I," she added honestly, brushing egg white off her sketch.

"I can't imagine either of you being much good at resisting," commented Saffron. "Not like Sarah and me, who are cultivating hearts of stone (probably reaction). Was your mother an unresisting kind of person, Sarah?"

"Don't know," said Sarah, licking cake mixture off her fingers. "We'll ask her at her birthday party if you like. So, yes, rich Italian living in Venice, all we need now is a name."

"We'll search the house while this cake is in the oven," said Saffron. "There must be stuff hanging about that came from Italy when I did. Letters and things . . . Do you know where they are, Eve?"

Eve, suddenly looking noticeably less happy, paused before she answered. "There's a whole box full of that sort of thing on top of my wardrobe. Bill sorted it out and put it there years ago. I've never looked; it felt too much like prying, but somehow I don't think you'll find a rich Italian there, Saffy. Why not leave it a bit longer?"

"Eve!" said Sarah. "Don't you want to know who Saffy's father is?"

"Not really," admitted Eve, as she began to pack up her drawing things. "Actually, not at all! Look at the time! I must be off to the horrible hospital . . . Well, of course it's not horrible, but I am always so afraid I will catch a glimpse of B-L-O-O-D. And faint. Who's looking after you, Rosy Pose?"

"I'm looking after myself," said Rose.

"Sarah and I will take her swimming," said Saffron, "as soon as we've finished this cake and . . ." She hesitated, searching for the right words.

"Tracked down your rich Venetian papa?" suggested Sarah. "If you eat any more of those cherries, Rose, you'll be too drunk to come swimming."

"I don't want to go swimming," objected Rose.

"You have to learn," Sarah told her, producing an enormous baking tin and beginning to ladle it full of cake mixture. "Me and Saffy checked out Venice on the Internet. It looks like the easiest place in the world to drown."

"I'm not going to drown," said Rose, rather indistinctly because she was sucking a cake spoon, "because I'm not going to go there. So. I think this cake is going to be too chocolately."

"Nothing can ever be too chocolatey, can it, Eve?" asked Sarah.

"Of course not," said Eve, but she glanced a little doubtfully into the cake tin.

"What on earth have you been making?" asked Caddy, coming in and peering over Sarah's shoulder. "It looks absolutely poisonous!"

"It does, but it isn't," Sarah told her. "At least I really hope not, because it's Mum's birthday surprise! And it's all finished except we have to fill it with cream and cherries, and ice it with fudge, and stick on forty-five candles. There'll be room; I doubled the recipe. I'll just sprinkle on our surprise secret ingredient and then someone can shove it in the oven for me."

"I always say a little prayer when I put cakes in the oven," remarked Eve, as she stooped to kiss Rose good-bye.

"What do you say?"

"I say, 'Please, God, don't let me forget I've put

that cake in the oven.' Bye-bye, everyone! Lovely rose, Rose!"

"From Michael," said Rose, and Caddy groaned and said, "Don't talk about Michael! I'm sure I've lost that frightful ring, and when I telephoned him to ask him if it was insured, he said, 'You can't put a price on love. Of course it's not insured; I never thought you'd take it off!' What's the matter, Rose?"

Rose was frantically searching the pocket where she knew she had put the ring. Then she searched the one where she knew she hadn't. Then she rushed upstairs and groveled all over her bedroom floor, found it, stuffed it back in her pocket, and lay on her bed with her eyes tight shut, waiting for her heart to stop pounding. She discovered she felt sick.

"Cherries," diagnosed Saffron, coming up to see what was the matter with her, and Rose, who had forgotten about the cherries, immediately felt better. She was quite happy to give up eating brandy-soaked cherries (which had never come her way before and weren't very likely to do so again), but she didn't want her secret life of crime to make her sick. Not when it was going so well.

Only I mustn't lose Caddy's ring again, she

thought. *That's twice already it's got out of my pocket!*

To prevent it from happening a third time, she took off her shorts and pushed the ring down to the very bottom of the pocket. Then, with a needle and thread, several drops of blood, and some rather heavy breathing, she sewed the top of the pocket shut.

Indigo banged on her bedroom door (which she was leaning on as a security precaution) just as she was finishing.

"Want to come with me to the music shop?" he called.

"To see if they've heard from Tom?" asked Rose eagerly.

"I suppose we could ask that. I bet they haven't, though. I need some new guitar strings, that's why I'm going."

"I'll come," said Rose, scrambling back into her shorts and opening the door. "Then I won't have to go swimming! Good! Is that smell Sarah's cake?"

"Yes," said Indigo, following her down the stairs. "And they are both on their knees in front of the oven door trying to see through the little glass window. They look like they are waiting for it to explode."

"That's because we *are* waiting for it to explode,"

said Sarah, overhearing him. "It's got a layer of popcorn on the top. We're waiting for it to pop."

"Was that the surprise secret ingredient?" asked Rose.

"Yes, but nothing is happening. Perhaps it isn't hot enough. I'll turn the oven up higher again."

"I wish I could see it pop," remarked Rose.

"You don't have to come with me," Indigo told her.

"I want to," said Rose.

Out in the street she hopped along beside Indigo very contentedly. She liked the music shop. During his stay in England, Tom had haunted it, and Rose had haunted it with him. The owner liked musicians, however young and penniless. Week after week Tom had been allowed to come and try out the black guitar that he longed to buy, while Rose sat and listened, or prowled among the dusty instruments at the back, or fiddled with the perpetual supply of special offers on the counter. Rattles shaped like eggs for shaking out a rhythm. Bookmarks made from old sheet music. A jumbled box of guitar picks, all different colors. These things had become a part of Rose's world, and she did not know how much she had missed them until she was on the way back to see them again.

"Let's hurry," she suggested, and for a few minutes they did, but they soon slowed down. Even for Rose it was too hot to run. Every morning, it seemed, the heat grew unbearable slightly earlier than the day before.

They were glad to turn out of the glare and in at the entrance of the music shop. It was good to hear the familiar jangle of the bell above the door; the smell was the same too, polish and wood and old dust. The box of guitar picks was in its place on the counter, the same posters decorated the walls. For a moment Rose expected Tom's voice to call, 'Hello, Permanent Rose!' from the shadows at the back of the shop.

Then the magic faded. It was not the same. A red electric guitar hung where the black one had been. Tom's stool was pushed against a wall and was stacked with copies of dog-eared catalogs. A set of drums filled the corner where she used to sit and listen.

The owner recognized them both, and he asked about Tom almost at once. Rose heard Indigo admitting that they did not know how he was, they had not heard if he got the black guitar safely back to America, they had not heard a word.

"Have you?" Indigo asked, more for Rose's sake than because he thought it might possibly be true, and the owner said, "No. No. No, I haven't. No," and shook his head.

Rose, who had looked around to hear his answer, turned away again.

"Well, never mind," said Indigo, and asked about guitar strings.

It seemed that there were very many different sorts of guitar strings, and since the music shop owner was the sort of person who liked things to be done as well as possible, he took down set after set and explained their differences. And all the time he was doing this, taking down packets of guitar strings and showing Indigo exactly how to put them on (with the help of a terrible old wreck of a guitar from the back of the shop), he talked about Tom.

"He was a proper player," he said, watching critically as Indigo threaded a string and knotted it carefully. "Not like some that come in here. Wanting the latest electric models and no more idea how to play them than my cat . . . That's right. . . . Now up to the tuning peg . . . You'll be doing it with your eyes shut before you know where you are. It's just a knack . . . No more idea than my cat, but money no object . . . Good. . . . Try another . . . You want them to look tidy. . . . He was a proper player, that boy . . ."

As Rose listened, the shop seemed to become a little less empty. If there was no Tom about anymore, at least there was a memory of him. A good memory too. She stirred the guitar picks in their battered box and felt the familiar enjoyment of their smooth, sliding shapes and colors. There were even a couple of hologram ones. Sometimes she had wished Tom would chose one of those, but he never did. He chose the translucent reds.

Rose sifted one out with her fingers. It fitted like a lucky charm into the palm of her hand.

Meanwhile, back at the Casson house, the heat in the kitchen had become tremendous and the popcorn was still refusing to pop.

"Maybe if we go away and pretend we don't care, it will start," Sarah said hopefully.

"Perhaps," Saffron agreed, so they had turned up the heat a little higher still, and left the cake to explode in private. Now they were in Eve's bedroom, ransacking the top of the wardrobe.

"There are about *twenty* boxes up here!" said Saffron, who had climbed up on a chair to hunt. "All covered with dust and thrown-away underwear!"

"Oh, you Cassons are so artistic and dysfunctional and cool, it's not fair," said Sarah. "Stop showing off and chuck them down!"

"All of them?"

"Why not?"

"Okay then," said Saffron, and began passing down boxes, which Sarah pulled open with comments like, "Baby shoes again!" or "Christmas tree lights and some odd socks," or "LPs. Look! Real vinyl!"

In the middle of all this there was a knock at the back door.

"Nobody who matters would knock," said Saffron. "Ignore it. They'll go away."

Whoever it was did not go away. Instead they knocked again, and then they started calling, "Hey! Hey!" in a breathless and creaky voice until at last Sarah gave in and peered out the window to see who it was.

"It's that boy," she said. "David or something. The fat one from the gang that got Indigo."

"Oh, him," said Saffron. "We don't want him. Close the window before he notices you."

But it was no good. The knocking and the calling continued until at last Sarah was forced to stick her head out of the window again and remark, "It can't be anything important."

This startled David so much he fell over backward on the doorstep.

Sarah withdrew her head and continued unpacking boxes.

"Gone?" asked Saffron.

"Soon," said Sarah, but she was wrong.

"Hey!" called David. "Don't go! There's something burning really badly in your kitchen!"

"What's he saying?" asked Saffron.

"Says something's burning in the kitchen."

Saffron tried but failed to not look alarmed by this information.

"Stop worrying," said Sarah. "It can't be the cake. The recipe said it would take an hour and a quarter to cook. And I doubled everything so that's two and a half hours. It hasn't had anything like that long." She stuck her head out of the window again and said, "You can just smell baking. Good-bye."

However, David seemed determined not to be ignored. He shouted, "Help! Help!" and hammered so hard that Saffron climbed down from her chair, opened the bedroom door, and stood and sniffed at the top of the stairs. Something certainly was burning in the kitchen.

"I can hear bangs," she said. "I'm going to look."

"Really!" said Sarah crossly, bumping on her bottom down the stairs after Saffron. "That's just pandering to him! It's only a bit of popcorn popping. It pops at 345 degrees Fahrenheit (I looked it up on the Internet). The cake is baking at 355. (Ish.) (Maybe a little more!) Anyway, obviously it's going to go off! It is a controlled experiment . . ."

The kitchen was full of smoke.

"Chocolate vapors!" said Sarah, coughing. "Delicious! I am a fantastic cook!"

By this time Saffron had the oven door open. She pulled out Sarah's baking tin and Sarah shut her eyes and said, "I am going for a puffy-popcorn-chocolate-soufflé effect, which Mum will love . . ." She unsquinted her eyes for a fraction of a second and took a quick look. The cake popped one final pop and then gave a sigh like a dying animal and sank.

"It's meant to do that," said Sarah, quickly shutting her eyes once more. "Don't show it to David, Saffron, or I'll never speak to you again!"

"Puffy-popcorn-chocolate soufflé, or carbonated exploding swamp?" inquired Saffron, waving the cake tin under her nose. "Probably which?"

"Swamp," admitted Sarah, so Saffron put it down, opened the door a tiny crack, and said, "Thank you for your concern. Everything is under control. You will find Indigo at the music shop with Rose, if you run."

David hung around for a few minutes after the door closed. He could hear shrieking. He recognized it as the shrieking of people who are laughing so much they are in pain, so he was not alarmed.

Chapter Seven

DAVID FELT GOOD.

Even though he was on the wrong side of a closed door, he felt good. He realized that the wild laughter on the other side of the door was at least partly caused by the fact that he, David, had blundered unexpectedly onto the scene, but he still felt good.

I made them come and stop whatever was burning, thought David as he hurried (he did not run, running would have killed him) along the road to town, and he smiled so hugely that passersby noticed him. They saw a big lumpy boy in a baggy white T-shirt, enormous denim shorts, desperate trodden wrecks of sneakers, and a smile on his hot, round face like the smile on the face of the moon.

A mirrored shop window caught his eye, and suddenly curious, he stopped to look.

It was a long time since David had last looked in a mirror, so long that he did not quite know what to expect. The red face that looked back at him could have been any stranger.

That is me, thought David, and the reflection looked a little interested, as if mildly surprised to be recognized.

What do I look like to people? wondered David. *I look . . . I look like a big . . . I look like a big, hot . . . I look like a big, hot,* ridiculous *person!*

That was such a good description that David smiled again, and his reflection smiled triumphantly back. They were briefly noticed by someone tall and good-looking sauntering along the street behind. That person paused for a moment to advise in an amused voice, "You should get a hat, mate!" and then passed on out of sight.

David nodded. It was true that a hat would help. In it he would look like a big, hot, ridiculous person wearing a hat.

He went on his way again, still smiling.

I did the right thing, he thought. *Making the girls stop that burning. The right thing.*

That was why he was so happy. It was because he had found the right thing to do at last.

All his life David had been confused about what

was the right thing to do. For the first ten or eleven years it had been fairly simple—he had been a noisy nuisance. Nothing else. But then more had been demanded of him. The right thing to do (and it had seemed exactly right because he was so effortlessly good at it) was to be a thug. A tormentor of isolated people. The means to block a doorway. The weight behind a heavy knee. And often much worse. Even now David could not put into actual words some of the things he had done when the right thing to be was a thug. It still surprised him that no one had died.

It was at this period of his life that he had first met Indigo, and because of Indigo, Saffy and Sarah and Tom and Rose. He did not suppose that Rose would ever forgive him.

After it had dawned on David that being a thug was not the right thing, he had become very humble. A humble admirer of Tom and Indigo, particularly Indigo, whom he had tormented most of all. He tried to be like him. He bought a skateboard and terrified himself learning to balance on it. He listened to Indigo's sort of music, although it filled him with a sort of baffled pain. For a very short time he took to self-consciously carrying a book around. Once he had even visited the music shop and pretended he was thinking of buying an electric guitar. This had been a terrible experience. He had been subjected to such a barrage of impenetrable and humiliating questions (for example, "What sort of music do you want to play?") that he had escaped as soon as possible and promised himself he would never go back.

He did not quite understand why he was going back now, except that Indigo was there, and Rose. He wished he could make Rose take notice of him.

David reached the music shop just at the moment when Rose palmed the red guitar pick. He looked through the window and saw her do it, and she saw him see her. Her eyes met his in defiant hatred, and then she abruptly turned her back. She looked so fierce that for a moment or two he hesitated about going inside, but then he pushed open the door anyway.

"Hi, David!" said Indigo at once.

"Hello," said David. "I went around to your house, and the girls told me you were here."

"How's their cake?" asked Indigo.

"Burning," said David, and although Rose refused to look at him, Indigo laughed, and so did the shop owner.

David laughed too, and gave a sigh of relief. The music shop suddenly felt a much less frightening place. For one thing, his status as a friend of Indigo's changed the shop owner's attitude completely. He offered to get down electric guitars for him to try, and when David said, "Oh no, it's all right, I don't know nothing about them. I just wondered!" he said, "No harm in wondering," quite civilly. For the first time in his life David felt like a real person. Someone like Indigo, who could visit a shop without being suspiciously watched by the owner all the time he was there. The sort of person who could be left in a room with someone else's set of drums and not give it a wallop.

It was a truly magnificent set of drums. It was the sort of drum set no mother would ever allow her son to keep in his bedroom. David looked at it and looked at it and the more he looked the more he thought he was born to be a drummer.

He reached out one finger and touched the largest drum.

Indigo and the shop owner, who had been watching him all the while, burst out laughing, because it was such a very small touch for such a big person and such a big drum.

Rose did not laugh because she was not there.

The music shop door rang a bell when it opened, and it rang the same bell when it closed, but if you opened it very gently, not the full way, and if you slid cautiously out of the gap and left it balanced where it was, not open and not shut, it made no sound at all.

All the time David had been in the music shop Rose had been seething with anger. She had hated David being there. Indigo had been engrossed in learning how to string a guitar. The shop owner had been busy teaching him. David had appeared to be in a sort of dumb trance in front of a drum kit. Rose slipped out the door.

"She's run off home!" said Indigo, when at last they noticed she was gone, and forgetting his packet of guitar strings, he called his thanks to the shop owner and ran off after her.

"You see her safe!" called the music shop owner as he watched him go and, turning to David, he said, "You'll take his strings for him?"

"Yes," said David. "I'll try and catch them up."

"You do that," agreed the music shop owner, and

as David set off into a lumbering jog, he thought, *That may not be such a bad boy as he looks.*

The first person that summer to look at David and think, *That may not be such a bad boy as he looks,* had been Indigo. The second was the stranger who had told him to get a hat. Now there was a third.

With Rose, a few perfect words from *Le Morte D'Arthur* went a long way because she hardly ever read anything. With David it was the same. A little bit of respect, just the sound in a voice, raised him higher than he had ever been before. He felt suddenly light as air, and he gave a sort of elephantine hop, and turned and waved back at the music shop owner, smiling his newly acquired enormous smile.

"Hmmm," said the music shop owner thoughtfully as he watched him from the doorway, and he raised a hand back in salute.

"Certainly got the build for a drummer," he said.

Saffron and Sarah put the exploded carbonated swamp in the garden to cool, opened all the doors to let the smell out of the house, and went back to looking for the box Eve had described. They found it at last, right at the back of the wardrobe.

"Are you sure that's the right one?" Sarah asked when she saw it. "I thought it would be huge."

But it was definitely the right one. It was labeled LINDA in Bill's handwriting and taped up very neatly all around, as only Bill would bother to tape a box. They took it out in the garden and sat down in the shade of Eve's shed and looked at it.

"You don't have to open it," said Sarah. "We could just put it back."

"No, we couldn't," said Saffron. "Not now that we know it's there." And she peeled off the tape.

She was disappointed from the moment she opened it. The box was not even full. There were a few photographs, a bundle of letters, a tatty address book, and two blue notebooks that had been used as diaries.

Saffron turned over the photographs. Bill and Eve, Linda herself waving from the stony walls of Siena, several of a baby. "Caddy," guessed Saffron, and sure enough there was Eve's writing on the back, "Caddy 14 weeks," "Caddy, 2nd birthday," perhaps a dozen all together.

"She must have had photographs of you," said Sarah.

"Oh yes, she did," agreed Saffron. "I have an

album full in my bedroom. Eve made it for me years ago. It's full of pictures of me, and my mother, too."

"No men?"

"No."

"What about the notebooks then?"

Saffron picked them up and looked at them. She said, "If I kept a diary and someone read it when I was dead, I would hate it."

"We won't read it then," said Sarah.

"No. We're reading it. It's got to be read."

"Which would be worse? Family reading it, or a complete stranger?"

"Family," said Saffron at once.

"Better let me look at it then, if it's really got to be read. You do the letters."

The letters were all from Eve, and Eve had not changed.

Darling Linda,
I am writing this in my shed . . .

Darling Linda,
You are so lucky; no fireflies here! I have been making charcoal in the

oven ON PURPOSE this time! With willow sticks. Caddy loved it. There are little black handprints all over the house . . .

Darling Linda,
Thank you, thank you, thank you.
Don't tell Bill . . .

"There is nothing in these diaries, Saffy," said Sarah soberly. "Not a word. They are too early. The last one ends months before you were born."

"How many months?"

"Nearly a year. And anyway, they are not chatty diaries . . . Well, the first one starts off chatty, but they get less and less like that, just appointments and birthday reminders, stuff like that. No names. Doodles . . . There are more of those than anything. Look!"

The doodles were tiny sketches. A leaf. A star. A glimpse of a building, a face.

"She was good at faces," said Sarah. "Look, there's Eve and Bill!"

"Perhaps she was homesick," said Saffron, and

from the address book this seemed to be more than likely. Nearly all the addresses that Saffron's mother had bothered to write out properly were English ones. It was a mess, like Caddy's address book, full of crossed-out names and telephone numbers.

"Yesterday Rose asked Caddy if Michael was in her address book," Saffron told Sarah, as she turned the pages, "and Caddy said of course he wasn't. She only wrote in the people she thought she might possibly forget. . . . Do you think my mother thought she might possibly forget my father?"

"No."

"Neither do I," said Saffron, and all at once she scooped everything up, letters and notebooks together, and pushed them back in the box.

"Whoever my rotten father was," she said angrily, "he didn't care about me."

Sarah let her do it: scoop them in all crumpled, wedge on the lid with a smack, push the box petulantly away, and sit with her face buried in her knees.

"Come on, Saffy!" she said at last. "Hearts of stone!"

"Oh, shut up!" snapped Saffron.

"Who wants a rich Venetian papa, anyway? How pretentious!"

"I didn't want a rich Venetian anyone! I just wanted to know who my father was."

"I know," said Sarah. "It's tough. Tough, but not unbearable."

"What do you know about unbearable?"

"Ho," said Sarah, pleased. "What do I know about unbearable? Guess what? I would swap having a father for fully functional legs!"

"You wouldn't!"

"Some days I would."

"Your father is lovely!"

"Yes, he is. So are your legs. It's a pity we can't share. Some days one of us could have the legs, and other days the father . . . Only we'd probably fight."

"You do talk some rubbish," said Saffron, smiling a bit.

"I know. And speaking of rubbish, we have to make another birthday cake. Can I count on your support?"

"What, today?"

"Yes. Birthday tomorrow."

"Oh, please not, Sarah! It's much too hot to begin cooking again!"

"I know. It's just a bad day. Your mother must have wanted to forget who your father was and got rid of the evidence. My cake exploded in front of that horrible David. Caddy is falling apart at the thought of marrying Michael. Indigo's best friend has dumped him. Rose waits for letters every day and never gets them. . . . You're all right though, Saffy! You have me! And all the rest of them! And don't forget, you still have Bill! Fully functioning legs *and* lovely, wicked old Bill!"

For some reason this made them laugh and laugh.

After Rose had sneaked out of the music shop, she had not gone home. Instead she had trudged the familiar way to Tom's grandmother's house. Despite everything Indigo had said the night before, she had not been able to get out of her head the idea that someone had been there.

Who? wondered Rose. *A friend of Tom's grandmother, passing by? Someone lost? A burglar?* That was a scary thought.

But I can run, Rose told herself. *Very fast! Faster than grown-ups. Anyway, a burglar would have finished burgling by now. And what if it was Tom?*

What if Indigo was wrong? What if, somehow, Tom had come back?

"Tom," said Rose, and saw a picture of his face in her mind.

Of course, when she arrived there was no one. The house was shut up and silent, and the garden was just empty. Emptier than it had been before somehow, and not even scary this time. Very hot.

Hotter than home, thought Rose, under the smothering darkness of the yew trees. The yews seemed to have sucked every drop of moisture out of the ground around them so that the lawn was split with gaping cracks as if the world was falling apart. There was a smell, too.

Suddenly Rose remembered the cat and looked across to where it had been, stretched out under the hedge.

It was still there.

I hope it is not dead, thought Rose, but it did not look dead. There was a little breathing movement about it. *Asleep,* decided Rose. Maybe that is its favorite place in the sun. She began to go across to look at it, but as she got closer she stopped.

The smell was the cat. Sweet and rank and dreadful, and the movement she had noticed . . .

"I'm going home!" cried Rose aloud. She turned in panic, and as she turned, a flash of silver fell at her feet, rolled into one of the open cracks of the lawn, and disappeared.

Caddy's ring! Rose's hand flew to her pocket. It was still sewn up. Sewn up tight all the way across, but the hard little lump where the ring had been was gone.

"How can it have gone?" asked Rose, bewildered, not knowing how easily a large brightly cut diamond can rub a hole in a soft cotton pocket. "And where?"

"Down the crack beside the cat," said Rose to Rose, and she said, "I can't go near that cat again. I can't." But bravely she took a step nearer.

The smell was appalling.

"Don't look at the cat!" Rose told herself as she stooped down to peer into the crack.

Caddy's diamond had never looked more like a star. A star wedged in a gap in the earth, just out of reach.

I need a stick, thought Rose. A little stick.

Then she froze.

There was a sound in the garden. And the star

went suddenly dim. Also there was a new smell, sweat and chocolate.

"I knew you'd be here," said David, smiling, blotting out the light with his shadow.

When Indigo was around, or Saffron and Sarah, reducing David to his constituent parts (oil and pulp, said Sarah), when there was anyone at all within reach, Rose did not know she was afraid of David. She knew she was bored, repelled, resentful, disgusted, but she did not know she was afraid.

David did not know either. Not until Rose, trapped between himself and the terrible thing that the cat had become, chose the cat.

"You go away!" said Rose, backing toward the cat.

"Rose!"

"I'm not scared of you!" Rose shivered, as if it were cold instead of boiling hot.

"Rose!"

"You do anything to me, and see what happens to you! Indigo will kill you. Saffy and Sarah will. Caddy. Tom. Tom will come back and kill you!"

David took a step closer.

"What are you going to do?" cried Rose.

Chapter Eight

CADDY HAD BEEN LOSING HER RING ALL SUMMER, BUT NEVER before had it vanished so completely. She had searched for it for hours and hours. It was beginning to feel like a nightmare.

"It is in my room; I know it is," she told herself. "It was in its box. I remember thinking I would keep it there for a while. I know I did not put it on!"

Caddy searched every inch of her room. She stripped the bed. She emptied every drawer and box and pocket. As she searched, she chanted to herself, a sort of moaning, regretful lament. "If only Michael didn't want to *actually* marry me. I don't mind doing practically *anything* so long as I know when it's going to end! But you *don't* know when marrying is going to end . . ."

She began shaking a pile of magazines by their middles, in case the ring should have accidentally been folded between two pages.

"It carries on and on until you wear out. Or one of you gives in and runs away . . ."

She found her old school bag, unopened for three years, and tipped everything onto the floor.

"Perhaps I swallowed it in my sleep," she said. "I should go to the hospital and get an X-ray. But they would think I was a fool."

"I am a fool," said Caddy. "I don't know what to do. If I had the ring, I think I would know what to do. I am tired of dodging poor Michael."

Just as she said that, the telephone rang, and it was Michael.

"Why did you want to know if it was insured?" he asked.

"I only wondered. No special reason."

"I'm coming around."

"No, don't!" said Caddy, panicking. "I am going out to work in ten minutes."

Michael said he would be there in five minutes and would stop for four and a half. Unless Caddy didn't want to see him.

"Of course I want to see you, Michael darling!" cried Caddy. "What about tomorrow?"

"What about it?"

"By then I might . . ." Caddy paused. "I mean it might . . ."

"Go on?"

"Not be so hot . . ." said Caddy desperately.

"Caddy," said Michael. "Since when did our relationship depend on the weather forecast? I'll be there in three minutes."

Caddy spent the three minutes putting on every ring she could find in the house in the hope of being able to wave a vaguely sparkling hand at Michael without him noticing exactly what was causing the sparkle. There were several silver ones belonging to Saffron, a piratical-looking thumb ring shaped like a skull, and a worn gold signet ring that they had decided at the last minute not to bury with Caddy's grandfather. It was a fairly hopeless plan, and it did not work for even thirty seconds because the first thing Michael did when he arrived was grab both of Caddy's hands and demand, "Where is it? Lost? Or chucked away?"

"Of course not!"

"If you don't like it, come into town and choose one that you do."

"The one you chose was perfect! It looked like a star."

"Then why are you crying?" asked Michael.

In the parched garden, with Rose and the cat and the cracks in the lawn, David was crying too.

At least, thought the astonished Rose, he looked like he was crying. Tears were pouring down his cheeks, faster than he could rub them away.

They had begun when Rose screamed.

I didn't mean to scream, thought Rose, watching in fascination the silent flood that was flowing over David's face.

But the words had come out like a scream: "What are you going to do?"

Then David had known what he looked like to Rose. Not the big, hot, ridiculous person he had seen in the shop window. Much, much worse than that.

"I'm not going to do *anything,* Rose!" he said at last. "I came here *to look after you!* I guessed you'd come here. You did before. Come away from that cat!"

"What?"

"Come away from that cat. It needs burying."

That was so true and so sensible it brought Rose

back to the real world again, and there was nothing scary anymore. Only a dry garden, and a poor dead cat, and David wiping the last of the flood away.

She remembered something he had said a minute ago. "How do you know I came here before?"

"I saw you. Yesterday. I saw you on your own in the street. I followed after you to see if you were all right. In case you were going into town to steal stuff again!"

Rose, who was still holding the guitar pick, felt herself go bright red.

"But you came here instead."

"Did you watch me?"

"Yes."

"I knew someone was here. That's why I came back today. In case it was Tom."

"*Tom!*"

"He *might* have come back," said Rose unsteadily.

David had a sudden longing to find Tom for Rose. To produce him with a flourish and announce, "Rose, I got you Tom!"

Like a hero.

I would if I could, he thought, and then his brain went scattering on to imagine it all. David the hero, and Rose's astonished admiration. "David!" she would exclaim. . . .

If I really did it, thought David. *If somehow I could do some brave, amazing magic and get him right here, Rose would not give one thought to me.*

He sighed and looked down at her. She was poking in a crack in the lawn with a stick, ungratefully unaware of David's heroic dreams.

"Come on," he told her. "I'll take you home."

"I can't go home," said Rose, not looking up, and jabbing away with her stick. "I've lost something down this crack. It's going deeper and deeper."

Her stick broke, and she threw it crossly away and it hit the cat, causing a humming cloud of flies to rise and then resettle like a shadow.

"You've *got* to come away from that cat," said David, suddenly taking control. "You'll get germs! What is it you've lost? Let me look!"

To his surprise Rose did as she was told, moving away so he could get down and see. "It's something I dropped," she told him. "A ring."

Not for a moment did it occur to David that it might not be Rose's ring. He knew little girls had things like that. They got them out of Lucky Bags, or free from the front of comics, or in princess sets from toy shops. Beads and bracelets, rings and hair clips, he had seen them dozens of times in his shoplifting days. He assumed this was just another, worth nothing to anyone except Rose.

"Have you got to have it?" he asked.

"Yes," said Rose.

"It's gone too deep to reach with bits of stick. Leave it for now."

"I can't."

"You'll have to. They'll be worrying about you at home. I'll come back and get it for you, if you like."

"How?"

"With a spade or something. Something to dig with."

"What if anyone sees you?"

"I'll come when it's dark. With a flashlight."

"What about the cat?"

"I'll bury it."

"In the dark? On your own? Will you really?"

"Yes."

"And not tell anyone?"

"No."

"And give the ring straight to me?"

"Yes."

"Promise?"

"Promise," said David.

When Michael had gone away, Caddy did not go to work. She went into the kitchen and looked at Bill's little Post-it on the fridge.

ANY TIME, DARLINGS, ALWAYS
WITH LOVE,
DADDY

Any time? reflected Caddy. *I wonder if he really meant it. Perhaps I could visit him. I think I need to get away for a while.*

Michael telephoned and said, "You sold it?"

"NO!" shouted Caddy, and slammed down the phone.

Then Saffron and Sarah appeared and started constructing another cake, and the mess from the new one was even worse than the mess from the old.

"Why can't you buy a cake?" demanded Caddy, and they said, "What's the matter with you? We are not hurting you! Pass the eggs! Don't put your elbow there! Why does Rose have to leave heaps of crayons on every surface in the house?"

"Where *is* Rose?" demanded Indigo, coming in at that moment.

"You had her!" said everyone. "Have you lost her *again*?"

Before Indigo could reply, the telephone rang.

"You gave it away!" said Michael.

"You are being totally unreasonable!" snapped Caddy, banging the receiver down. "Saffron! There is disgusting chocolate goo all over this table!"

"Moan, moan, moan," said Saffron. "No wonder Michael dumped you! Mind that box!"

"Michael hasn't dumped me!" shouted Caddy, not minding the box, which fell to the floor just as Eve came through the door carrying the carbonated swamp (now cool).

"Everybody fine?" she inquired affectionately, seeming not to notice that Caddy and Saffron were angrily collecting letters and photographs from all over the room, and that the kitchen was in a state of chaos remarkable even by Casson standards. "I found this lovely cake outside, Sarah. You are so clever!"

"Eve," said Sarah, "it is hideous beyond belief."

"I always think that about mine, too," agreed Eve cheerfully, "but then I ice them and they are somehow transformed! . . . Oh."

All at once Eve realized what the papers were that lay strewn all about. She stooped and picked up a photograph. "Darling Linda," she said.

She was still looking at it when Rose came in, followed by David, who immediately trod first in a puddle of raw chocolate cake and next on a letter that had strayed across the room.

"Rose!" said Eve, kissing her. "And MarcusJoshPatrick . . . Which is it? I always forget."

"David," said David.

"David. *Look* where you are walking, David darling! Those things are very special."

"They are not," said Saffron loudly, over the sound of the telephone, which had begun again. "They are not remotely special! David can walk over them as much as he likes. There was nothing in that box worth saving so long! They made me feel like I was no one at all!"

"Oh, Saffy!" exclaimed Eve. "After darling Daddy saved them so carefully for you!"

"HE IS NOT DARLING DADDY!" shouted Saffron.

"Answer that telephone someone, for goodness' sake!"

David, feeling tremendously important, picked it up and said, "Hello, hello! This is David! To who do you want to speak?"

"To Caddy, of course," snapped Michael on the other end of the line. "Where is she?"

"She's here," said David. "Shaking her head. Saying no, no."

Caddy rested her head on a sticky patch of table and moaned.

"Ask her what she has done with her ring!"

"What ring?" said David.

Caddy grabbed the telephone from him and banged it down.

"What ring?" asked David again, goggling at her in surprise.

"My ring!" shouted Caddy, irritated beyond endurance. "My diamond and platinum engagement ring! That's what ring!"

"I've always liked the look of Michael," remarked Sarah to no one in particular. "I'll have him if you like, Caddy!"

"Oh, no you won't!"

"Well, you don't want him! Saffy doesn't want him! Rose is still getting over that loser Tom . . ."

Rose picked up the plastic bowl of cake mixture (double quantities of everything, beaten egg white just stirred in) and dumped it upside down on Sarah's head.

Caddy ran upstairs.

"If anyone wants me," said Eve, "I shall be in my shed. I am tired of being a single parent and I'm not surprised Bill left."

Sarah wiped chocolate cake mixture out of her eyes and said, "Sorry, Rose."

"I'm not," said Rose.

"Come on," said Saffron to Sarah. "I'll help you wash your hair."

Indigo made tea and took it out to Eve.

David and Rose found themselves alone together. David stared around. He felt as if something should be said to sum up this enormous mess of paper and shouting and cake mixture and emotion. It seemed wrong that it should pass with no comment at all.

Rose began to doodle in a patch of spilled flour. David groped in his mind for words that might do. He was dreadfully hot.

"It's the weather," he said, and was immediately surprised that the words he had wanted had somehow found themselves.

"Yes," agreed Rose.

"I wonder what will happen next."

"I don't know," said Rose.

Saffron and Sarah knew what had to happen next the moment they came down from the bathroom. It took two bottles of detergent, a whole roll of paper towels, a great deal of hot water, and ages of Radio 1 turned up very loud.

Caddy decided that what should happen next should be a phone call to London. She made it, and Samantha answered and listened with surprising understanding while Caddy tearfully explained that there were too many people at home, and that Michael came around every day, and that she, Caddy, could no longer bear the thought of being married to anyone, no matter how gorgeous, if it involved settling down forever with a house full of children and learning to cook. And when Caddy stopped talking to blow her nose, Samantha said sympathetically, "Perhaps you need to get away for a while."

"I do, I do," said Caddy, and afterward began to pack.

Indigo decided that food should happen next, and he cooked a strange meal of eggs and french fries and jam sandwiches for everyone except Rose who said she wanted oatmeal.

"Oatmeal," said Indigo, and cooked that, too.

Evening came, and David remembered his promise to Rose. He took himself off to visit his grandfather, whom he thought might lend him a spade.

Indigo went up and sat on the end of Rose's bed. She was curled up there, looking a little grubby and forlorn, but she brightened up at the sight of him.

"Thank you for the oatmeal."

"That's okay."

"Did you bring your book?"

"Yes."

"Is there any more in it about Lancelot that I haven't heard?"

"Yes. But a lot of it is sad."

"Sad a long time ago isn't the same as sad nowadays," said Rose.

"That's true. Well, then. Lancelot had a friend called Sir Ector. They fetched Sir Ector when Lancelot died. He was very fond of Lancelot. This is what he said."

Skipping bits to make it easier for Rose, Indigo read,

> **". . . and now I dare say," said Sir Ector, "thou Sir Lancelot, there thou liest, thou that were never matched of earthly knight's hand . . . And thou were the kindest man that ever struck with sword . . . And thou were the truest friend that ever bestrad horse . . . And thou were the goodliest person that ever came among press of knights."**

Indigo stopped and looked across at Rose.

"People were good at being friends in those days," said Rose. "Better than now."

"What about Saffy and Sarah?" asked Indigo. "They are friends like that. And Michael and you. And Tom. And David. I told you before, these days are the same as those days."

"Maybe." Rose was quiet for so long that Indigo thought she had fallen asleep, until she said drowsily, "Tell me their names. Lancelot and Kay. Percival. Arthur. The girl in the bath . . . What was she called?"

"Elaine. And there was Tristram and Isoud. Guinevere. Balin and Balan and Bagdemagus."

"Bagdemagus is a lovely name."

"Mmmm."

"And did they stay together always?"

"No, no. Some of them went off for ages and ages."

"Then what did the others do?"

"Waited till they came back."

"Like you and Tom?"

"Yep."

"I hate waiting," said Rose. "I would have gone to look!"

"Some of them did that, too."

"On their horses?"

"Yes. Or on their ships, maybe."

"I would need an airplane," said Rose.

Chapter Nine

ALL THAT WEEK THE HEAT HAD PILED UP LIKE A CURSE AND BY that Wednesday evening it was heavy with menace. Clouds began to build, shutting down the sky like a blanket. All afternoon people had said, "Listen! Was that thunder?"

Everywhere that David had ever itched began a simultaneous itching. Flies continually lost their sense of direction and hit him in the face. David ground his itches absentmindedly through his clothes as he walked along. He was thinking about spades, and he was rubbing his itches, and he was feeling, on the whole, pretty good. He always felt good going to his grandfather's house.

David's grandfather was (to David's continual surprise and pleasure) one of his very few relations who actually liked him. And, what was more surprising, had always liked him.

David's grandfather had stubbornly liked David all

through his shoplifting, bullying, bus-stop-vandalizing, banned-from-the-swimming-pool, disgraceful-and-not-too-distant days. Remarking, at each new awful revelation (none of which were ever spared him), "I dare say." And adding, as often as not, "He gets on very well with me." (Which was quite true, although surprising). Saying also, "He'll come through a very nice lad" (which, even more surprisingly, also seemed to be turning out to be true).

He'll not mind lending me a spade, thought David.

Even as he walked, the clouds grew darker and heavier. Then the light changed. It became yellow and alien. It was like the world was being given one last chance to look around before the sky fell down.

There were a few drops of rain and then nothing happened.

The rain excited people. They talked about it to each other. They noticed that it had an incredible smell, a mixture of spice and trash cans. They saw how it left reddish marks on white surfaces. A gusty wind had come up from the South. Someone said, "That rain was full of dust from Africa," and this exotic but unfounded story spread through the town by a network of old men at bus stops, shop girls traveling home, mothers lamenting the cost of back-to-school shoes, boys on skateboards, buskers packing up for the day, and swifts screeching low over the rooftops like mini–jet planes.

The news reached David as he sneaked out of his grandfather's shed, spade in hand, and bumped into his grandfather.

"That rain was straight from Africa," said David's grandfather, who had never been farther than London in his life. "Africa!" He took out a handkerchief, wiped a dusty splotch off the hood of his car, and inspected the faint redness almost reverently. "Think of that! And I dare say they could have done with it there themselves. What are you planning to do with my spade?"

"Bury a cat," said David, and his grandfather said, "Good lad," and let him go.

David made his way to Tom's old house in the darkness of the edge of a storm. It broke as he arrived, flinging the tops of the yew trees like black brooms against the sky. The rain began again and this time did not stop. David buried the sodden cat in a downpour of cold water that seemed wet beyond anything he had ever experienced, and he dug up Caddy's ring by pink and purple lightning.

• • •

Bill was not pleased when he heard that Samantha (in his absence) had told Caddy that his beautiful, shining, minimal-junk-containing London apartment (where even Samantha was only allowed to visit, not stay) was Caddy's for as long as she liked.

"She needs to get away for a while," said Samantha serenely. "I told her she must come at once."

"But we will be in New York!" Bill protested. "There will be no one to keep an eye on her. And all her friends will be around as soon as they hear she is in town! She will probably have half the under-twenty-fives in London sleeping on the floor!"

"Gosh, lovely!" said Samantha.

"Not to mention she is the most untidy person on the planet except possibly Eve . . ."

"I thought you said I was!"

"I shall not be able to relax for a minute!"

"Who goes to New York to relax?" asked Samantha.

"Samantha darling," said Bill crossly. "*I* am going because of my work but *you* are coming purely for pleasure! I was thinking of it as a sort of second honeymoon!"

"Second?" asked Samantha. "Second!" And she

added that she had been thinking of it as a free trip and shopping and she wasn't sure she wanted to go now at all.

Then they had a quarrel that Samantha won.

Afterward Bill sat down to write out a long list of instructions for Caddy on how not to destroy his flat. Followed by an equally long list of numbers she could ring for help if she accidentally did destroy it anyway. Samantha watched him writing with a very thoughtful expression on her face.

"Planning your shopping list?" asked Bill.

"No," said Samantha, and continued to look thoughtful.

David was very tired by the time he got home, and his mother was very cross. She said she'd been thinking any minute the police would ring up and she would have to go trailing out to collect him from the cells again. This was not fair at all; she made it sound like she had had to do this dozens of times, instead of only once. It hadn't been a cell even then (nothing so glamorous). It had been a waiting room.

David was too weary to point this out. He said, "Sorry, Mum," and staggered dopily up to bed. But before he went to sleep he took Rose's ring out of his sodden pocket (where it had become embedded in dissolving strawberry bubble gum), wrapped it in a paper handkerchief, and stowed it carefully under his pillow.

By morning the ring was part of a gluey bundle of tissue and mud and bubble gum. David took it to the bathroom and began to scrub it clean with his toothbrush. And as it grew cleaner, it began to dawn on him that this was a very solid, sparkly, real-looking sort of ring. It did not look like anything from a toy shop, or a comic, or even an exceptionally lucky Lucky Bag.

I wonder where Rose got it, thought David, and as if in answer he seemed to hear again the voices in the Casson kitchen the day before.

"What ring?" he had asked.

"My diamond ring!" Caddy had shouted. "My diamond and platinum engagement ring! That's what ring!"

"Crikey, Rose!" whispered David as he stared at the ring. He was torn between horror and admiration. He himself had never stolen anything that could touch it.

However, he knew exactly what would have happened if he had. He had not forgotten, and never would forget, the morning his own mother had turned him in to the police. Nor the hideous afternoon going through his bedroom, producing stolen goods. Nor the even worse day, spent apologizing to store managers. Or the weeks without pocket money that followed, the letters he had to write, and the horrible, still-present feeling of everyone knowing and remembering, every time they saw him.

The thought of these things happening to Rose was awful.

I should have stopped her as soon as I knew, he told himself. *I knew about that bottle of stuff. I saw her take that guitar pick. I let her get away with it, and now this! Diamond and platinum!*

And what else? wondered David.

That day the Early Morning Rose Delivery Service brought Rose a whole bunch of roses, damp and sweet from the rain the night before.

"We couldn't choose," said Michael. He was grinning at her out of the car window, and Rose saw that he had someone with him.

"My mate Luke," said Michael. "Luke, Permanent Rose! Luke's just back from a trip around the Pacific Ocean on his motorbike, Rose."

"Why didn't he sink?" asked Rose.

"The *edge* of the Pacific Ocean!" explained Michael, while Luke said, "I edge around edges! I'm doing Europe next."

"Oh," said Rose. "Do you go very close?"

"Close as I can get."

Rose had a quick vision of a motorbike steering very carefully around the extreme edge of a cliff.

"Can you swim?" she asked politely.

"Like a whale."

"Oh, good."

The postman was coming nearer and nearer. Usually he just strode by as if he didn't see her, but this morning he looked at Rose as if he had something to say. Rose held her breath and forgot about Michael and his friend, and motorbikes and whales.

And then suddenly he was past, just like all the other days. Rose stared after him in disbelief.

"One day Tom will write," said Michael gently.

"Saffy says he's forgotten about us."

"Never," said Michael. "Not possible! I should know!"

"Should you?"

"Think I haven't tried?" asked Michael, starting

his engine up. "How's Caddy? Bearing up? No, don't answer! I shouldn't have asked. Bye, Rosy Pose!"

Rose watched them go with relief. She was very glad she had not had to talk about Caddy, because Caddy was on her way to London. She had hugged them all as if she were going away forever, and wandered off to the railway station with her old backpack on her back.

"Let me drive you," offered Eve.

"No, no," said Caddy. "I've plenty of time, and walking is so peaceful. And I hate station good-byes! I'll come back as soon as I've thought what to do. Don't tell Michael the telephone number!"

She had gone, and two minutes later returned again.

"Promise to tell me the second it happens if anybody finds my ring?"

Rose did not like to think of that second good-bye.

She looked up from her roses, and there was David, puffing up the street toward her.

David had hurried all the way, thinking as he jogged and rested and jogged again, *What else has she taken?* As soon as he came up to Rose he dragged the diamond and platinum ring out of his pocket, held it in front of her eyes, and demanded, "What . . ."

Rose grabbed at the ring but missed.

". . . else?" asked David sternly. "Rose! You're going to get into such awful trouble, you don't know! That guitar pick! That bottle of stuff! Tell me the rest!"

"I won't tell you anything," said Rose.

"I'm telling Indigo then!"

"No!"

"I have to. Where is he?"

"Inside. Don't tell Indigo, *please,* David!"

Something in her voice caught David by surprise. He seemed to hear himself begging, "Don't tell Granddad, *please,* Mum!"

His voice softened a bit.

"I won't if you tell me what else you took."

"There wasn't anything else," said Rose sulkily. "Just that bottle of nail stuff. And little things from shops."

"You've got to give them all back!"

"I didn't bring them home. I just left them in the street."

"In the street?"

"*Tidily* in the street!" said Rose, as if that made it completely reasonable.

David gave up trying to understand. He said, "I'll give you back the ring and I won't tell Indigo if you promise never to take any more stuff. Not to leave in the street even. Not for anything. Promise?"

"All right."

"And you've got to give it all back! The bottle and that guitar pick and the ring!"

"What!"

"Starting with the ring! Go and take it in to your sister!"

"I can't."

"I will, then!'

"You can't either. She's gone. She's gone to London. She's catching the train. She went just a while ago."

"Walking or in her car?"

"Walking."

"Come on, then!" said David, and he grabbed Rose's hand and ran her down the street, right at the crossroads, past the park, over the town bridge, and then along the road that ran by the river and led to the railway station.

There were only two platforms. A train was in at the nearest one as they arrived, a huge intercity London-bound express. The doors were opened, and people were queuing to board. Caddy was one of them. David and Rose spotted her just as she heaved her backpack up the high step of the doorway and nimbly climbed up afterward.

“Quick!” said David, towing Rose across to the door. “Up you get! Run along until you find her, give her the ring, and get off at the next open door!”

“But I will have to tell her I took it!” wailed Rose.

“Serves you right! I’ll wait here!”

Before Rose could argue anymore, he had thrust the ring into her hand and boosted her up the step. And then he had to get out of the way because a whole family, with strollers and babies and dozens of bags, came crowding up to the doorway. Then there were two old ladies who moved terribly slowly, followed by a bunch of noisy boys with no luggage except skateboards.

David began to panic because he suddenly realized he had lost sight of Rose.

She was trapped in a narrow aisle full of cases and bags and legs sticking out from seats, surrounded by people twice her height, all pushing her forward. Every now and then she would get a glimpse of David’s face, bobbing up at a window for a moment. He was pointing to his watch, and then along the train, signaling to her that she should hurry.

It was impossible to hurry. It was impossible to do anything except inch forward very slowly. Rose began to feel very alone and frightened, but this did not last for long because she suddenly spotted Caddy at the far end of the carriage.

David was still bobbing up and down, but now his message had changed.

"Get off! Get off!" mouthed David through the window. And then there was a tremendous slamming of doors, and hissing of steam as the brakes came off, followed by the shrill whistling that meant the train was about to leave.

It would serve him right, thought Rose (who, with Caddy in sight, had stopped worrying completely). *It would serve him right if it started to move.*

It started to move.

Back at the Casson house Saffron and Eve were alone together. Eve had managed to find a photograph of Saffron with her mother that Saffron had not seen before. "It was put away with Granddad's things," Eve explained. "That's why I didn't have it when I was making your album. See how Linda is looking at you! She thought you were perfect, Saffy darling, which of course you were!"

"Did you truly never ask my mother about my father, Eve?"

"Of course I didn't! I know I am a tatty old hippie who lives in a shed, Saffy darling, but I do know better than to go around asking single mothers who the fathers of their children are!"

"You're not a tatty old hippie!" said Saffron, laughing.

"Well, there's much worse things to be! Now then, Saffy, I must dash! It's my last day at the hospital (although they have asked me to come back and do Accident and Emergency next summer) . . . (Horrible thought!) . . . (Kind, though). And I must say I have transformed Geriatrics and Children's beyond belief, although I know darling Bill would say it was 'not exactly Art' . . . Where's Rose?"

They searched for Rose in the house and the garden and the street. They rang Michael on his mobile, and Sarah at home. And then they put the phone down, and it rang itself, straight away.

.

The train that Caddy had boarded, that David had boosted Rose onto, that went all the way to London with only one stop, began to pick up speed. Rose had just time for one triumphant, Look-what-you-got-me-into glance at David (now reeling backward on the platform with his arms flung wide in despair), and then they were out of the station, and out of the town. She was still stuck in a slow-moving queue of people, but the aisle was gradually beginning to clear. She peered around someone's elbow to check on Caddy. She was still there. Rose waved, but Caddy had her eyes shut and did not wave back. Caddy was very tired. She had been awake most of the night, thinking about Michael and wondering what was the right thing to do if you loved someone tremendously but not quite enough to marry them, and had nevertheless accepted (and lost) a diamond and platinum ring.

It was a relief to be on the train. Caddy always enjoyed traveling on trains. She liked it because while you were on a train you were nowhere. No longer where you came from, and not yet where you were going. And (unless you had a mobile phone and were prepared to answer it) (which Caddy was not) nobody could get to you.

Caddy dumped her backpack on the opposite seat,

snuggled down in the corner, and fell fast asleep. She did not notice Rose tiptoeing toward her, moving the backpack, and sitting down in its place. She did not notice anything for ages and ages, not until they had nearly reached London. Then Rose, who had sat as quiet as a mouse, putting off the horrible moment when she would have to tell Caddy she had stolen her ring, joggled her apologetically and said, "Caddy, the ticket collector is coming."

At first Caddy only murmured, "Ticket collector . . . okay . . . right . . ." and groped for her backpack.

Then she woke up enough to realize that it was not where she had left it.

"Bag's gone," she said, squinting around with her eyes nearly shut and one hand up to screen the light from the window.

"Here," said Rose, pushing it toward her.

"Oh, thanks."

Caddy took the backpack and shut her eyes, clearly preparing to go to sleep again.

"Ticket collector," reminded Rose.

"Oh, yes," said Caddy dopily, and then she sat up, stared in disbelief, and asked, "Rose? No. Sorry. Dreaming . . . No, I'm not! ROSE!"

"Could you buy me a ticket?" asked Rose. "I'll pay you back when I'm rich."

"ROSE!" repeated Caddy. "ROSE!" And then the ticket collector was beside them, so she had to stop saying "Rose!" and find her ticket and buy another one for Rose, and by then she was awake enough to demand, "What on *earth* are you doing here?"

"I've been here all the time," said Rose, still putting off the horrible moment.

"Right from home?" asked Caddy, as if Rose might have somehow dropped in through the carriage roof halfway along the journey.

"Yes."

"Goodness!" said Caddy feebly.

"Go back to sleep if you like," suggested Rose hopefully.

Caddy did not go back to sleep. She stared at Rose with a puzzled, but not angry expression on her face. She appeared to be, if not actually thinking, at least coming around at last.

"Are you coming to Daddy's too, then?" she asked.

Rose was astonished. She had never planned such a thing. She had never planned any of it. David had blackmailed her into going to the station and shoved her on the train. And here she was. She said, "I suppose I am!"

She sounded so surprised Caddy started to laugh.

"Would you mind?"

"Not a bit, Rosy Pose!" said Caddy, still laughing. "As long as you don't talk to me about you-know-who."

"Who?"

"Darling Michael, who I promise I love, but that's not the same as wanting to marry! Goodness! Look! We're here!"

Caddy stood up and began heaving on her backpack, as if suddenly in the most frantic hurry. All around them, Rose noticed, their fellow passengers were doing the same. "Get your things, Rosy Pose!" ordered Caddy.

Rose did not have any things. Her only luggage was one diamond and platinum ring, rather warm and sticky from being clutched all the way to London. She started to stuff it in her pocket, remembered the hole, and said urgently, "Caddy, I do have to tell you one thing about Michael because—"

"Wait till we're off the train," said Caddy, pushing Rose into the aisle. "Come on! Off you get! Where have you gone? Rose?"

"I'm here!" said Rose, reappearing on the platform beside her. "Caddy, I've *got* to tell you one little very important bit about Michael because I've got . . ."

People were streaming all around. They did not seem to notice Caddy and Rose were together. They walked between them as if they were two strangers. Caddy lost Rose again, spun frantically around, grabbed her by the arm, and ordered, "Stay with me!"

"I am! Caddy, listen!"

"Shut up, darling Rose, while I look at this underground map and find out where . . . Rose! You've *got* to stop wandering off!"

"I wasn't! Please listen!"

"This way!"

"Why have we got to hurry? Stand still and listen!"

"Have you any change, Rose darling?"

"No. Caddy, I've got . . ."

"Just let me find a change machine that is working . . . Over here . . . Tickets . . . Which zone? *Rose*!"

For the first time ever Caddy saw how small Rose was. And losable. Somehow, in the moment Caddy's back was turned, Rose had been elbowed out of the change machine queue. And then she had stepped aside because someone said, "Excuse me, sweetie!" And then she had lost sight of Caddy, run around the back of the queue in the hope of finding her again, and suddenly become quite far away.

"Rose! Hold on to me and don't let go!" said Caddy angrily. "Now we've got to queue all over again!"

"But . . ."

"Don't say a word! Now come on! Across here! Please stay very close! It's terribly crowded!"

Rose gave up and hurried along with Caddy, clutching the ring so hard her fingers locked with cramp. On the underground train she tried again.

"Caddy!"

Caddy, who had pushed Rose into the only empty seat and was swaying beside her, shook her head and pointed to her ears to indicate she could not hear a thing. "Wait till we get there!" she shouted.

That was how Rose managed to get all the way to her father's front door without explaining to Caddy why she had gotten on the train in the first place.

Caddy was scrabbling through her bag.

"There's a number you key in for the door to open," she told Rose. "I've got it written down. . . . Yes, here!"

Rose was struck by a sudden thought.

"Do you think he will mind me coming?"

"Too late if he does," said Caddy heartlessly. "Anyway, he's going away himself tomorrow. Besides, you're here, aren't you? Why *are* you here, Rose?"

This was the horrible moment, arrived at last. Wordlessly Rose unclamped her fingers and held out the ring.

"Rose! Rose, where did you find that?"

"I didn't find it. I had it all the time."

"All the time I was looking for it?"

Rose nodded.

Caddy held the ring in the palm of her hand. It was far more beautiful than she remembered. It really was like a star.

"Michael thought you were going to give it back to him. You couldn't if you didn't have it."

Caddy was only half listening, turning the ring distractedly over and over in her hand.

"Poor Michael," she said. "He thinks I lost it. Or sold it. Or gave it away. I have to see him right now! I have to talk to him properly . . ."

She stopped and looked down at Rose. The thought of rushing her across London again was too much. Once had been enough. A desperate plan began to form in Caddy's head.

It is only till morning, she told herself. *I will come back then.*

"You're cross!" said Rose.

"I'm not! Not with you, anyway! I'm cross with myself." Caddy keyed in the security number she had found. "I've been awful to Michael . . ." The door buzzed to show it was unlocked. "In here, Rose. Daddy is at the top. Very posh. Elevator or stairs?"

"Stairs," said Rose.

"I'll just take you up, and make sure someone's in . . . And then . . . Don't look so worried, Rose!"

"Samantha will be there as well as Daddy, won't she?"

"Yes, but you'll be surprised. She's really nice. I thought I'd hate her, but I didn't. No one could."

Rose, temporarily silenced by the unfamiliarity of her surroundings, did not reply.

"Okay, Rosy Pose?" asked Caddy, half turning to look back at her.

Rose nodded and concentrated on trying to keep up with Caddy's long legs.

"Here we are! Ring the bell!"

The door was answered almost at once by a very pretty woman with long red curls.

"Caddy!" she exclaimed in a very pleased voice. "I thought I heard . . ."

"Darling Samantha," said Caddy, taking Rose by the shoulders and pushing her forward. "This is Rose! Would you be terribly kind and look after her (she gets lost very easily), because I must just dash back for a . . ."

"Of course I will look after Rose!" said Samantha at once. "Come in, both of you!"

"Not me," said Caddy hurriedly, stooping down to hug Rose. "Just Rose. Bye-bye, Rose darling. I'm not cross a bit! Thank you, Samantha!"

By the time Bill arrived, she was gone, flying down the stairs two at a time, racing for the front door.

"See you very soon!" she called, and then they heard the door slam behind her, and then she was gone.

"CADDY!" roared Bill.

Chapter Ten

BILL HAD BEEN BASED IN LONDON (AS HE LIKED TO PUT IT) since before Rose was born, in order to have peace and quiet in which to work. He did not encourage his family to visit him because they were not peaceful and quiet people. Eve had been there once or twice, long ago, and Caddy had barged in several times since she started college and became London-based herself, but Rose had never been there at all.

Rose peered curiously around her father as he stood blocking the doorway. She had a glimpse of high ceilings and shining floors and clear spaces between objects. It could not have been less like the Casson house, and yet she found herself feeling at home almost at once. Even before she stepped inside, she became embroiled in a very familiar situation.

The situation was this:

Successful, talented, tolerant-within-limits, first-to-admit-he-was-far-from-perfect, established artist,

i.e., Bill

vs.

Successful, talented, tolerant-within-limits, first-to-admit-he-was-far-from-perfect, established artist's

(i.e., Bill's)

Much-Loved Offspring

with

Person Who Should Have More Sense (usually Eve, but in this case Samantha) coming down illogically and disloyally on the Much-Loved Offspring's side.

"CADDY!" Bill roared down the stairwell as the street door slammed, but there was no reply and it did not open again.

"She's gone!" exclaimed Bill indignantly. "Gone! Who'd be a father!"

"That's not a very nice thing to say," remarked Rose.

"No," agreed Bill, and he gave a big sigh, raised

his hands to his face, smoothed out the creases on his forehead before they turned into wrinkles, and said, "Sorry, Rose!"

"It's okay."

"Well, give me a hug and tell me why you are here! Not that it isn't wonderful to see you . . . Your hands are very dirty, Rose!"

Rose put them quickly behind her back.

"I really do need to know what is going on. And aren't you going to say hello to Samantha?"

"Hello, Samantha," said Rose.

"Hello, Rose," replied Samantha. "I've wanted to meet you for ages and ages!"

Rose was looking around in amazement at her father's home. She said, "Our house must seem really scruffy to you!"

"Of course not!"

"And then when you come back here, you must feel really cool and posh, like a different person."

"Rose, where has Caddy gone and why are you here?"

"Rose," said Samantha, "why are you looking at me like that?"

"Sorry."

"But why?"

"I was only thinking of something Saffy said."

"Rose!" said Bill warningly.

"I wasn't going to tell her!" said Rose indignantly.

"Now you will have to!" said Samantha. "Does Saffron hate me, Rose?"

"When you have *quite* finished, Samantha," said Bill (doing the neck exercises he did to relieve stress), "it would be very nice if Rose took the time to answer my questions!"

Rose ignored him and turned to Samantha, whom she found herself liking already. "Saffy doesn't hate you!" she said kindly. "It's not like Daddy is her real father. All she said was that we should call you Stepmother and scare the pants off you. But don't worry. I won't."

"Thank you!"

"Anyway, you wouldn't be my stepmother unless you properly married Daddy. And murdered Eve. (That's Mummy.) Actually, I don't know if you would have to murder Eve in these days. (You would have in Indigo's olden days.) Anyway, it wouldn't be worth trying because we'd guess who'd done it . . ."

"Rose, be quiet!" ordered Bill.

"Better just to live in sin," advised Rose, taking no

notice of him. "Like you are doing," she added, wandering around the sitting room inspecting her father's possessions. "What's this?"

"It is a glass sculpture by a friend of mine," said Bill. "Please don't pick it up! Your fingerprints will mark the gold leaf. Rose, I need to know when Caddy will be back. I have rather a lot to go through with her."

"I don't know. She didn't say. Can't I just lift it up very carefully?"

"I'd rather you didn't," said Bill. "In fact, I'd rather you didn't touch anything with those hands! Samantha, do you think you could take Rose to the bathroom and see that she has a good wash?"

"I expect Rose can take herself to the bathroom," said Samantha. "Can't you, Rose?"

"Oh, all right. Where is it?"

"Haven't you been here before?" asked Samantha.

"No."

"Oh."

Samantha showed Rose where to go without further comment. When she returned, Bill was putting his sculpture away at the back of a high shelf that he hoped Rose could not reach.

"You will hurt her feelings."

"Samantha darling, whose side are you on?"

"Have I got to choose?"

Bill groaned and did some more wrinkle smoothing. Then Rose returned, less grubby but rather damp. She saw straight away that the sculpture had been moved in her absence, and anyone could see that her feelings were hurt.

"So," said Bill, giving her a kiss on the top of her head to cover up the fact that Samantha was right. "What about a drink, Rosy Pose, while we wait for Caddy? And you can get to know Samantha a little."

"All right," agreed Rose, and she asked Samantha politely, "are you an artist too?"

"Sort of. I work in graphic design."

"Not exactly Art!" Bill murmured to himself, as he fetched orange juice for Rose. "Now, Rose! What is the plan? Because Caddy knows I leave tomorrow. Are you staying here with her while I am in New York? Because I must say I don't . . ."

"NEW YORK!" exclaimed Rose. "NEW YORK!"

Suddenly the purpose of all the happenings of her summer became clear to her. The lonely shoplifting game, Indigo's unwelcome friend, David, Michael's roses, and Caddy's ring. They had brought her to London, and London, it seemed, was only a step from New York. Until that moment Rose had been almost as puzzled as Bill about why she was there, but now she knew. New York.

New York to Rose was where Tom was. That was all. If someone had said to her, "Draw New York," she would have drawn a picture of Tom. Under a sign that read NEW YORK.

The helpless feeling that had tormented her all summer was suddenly gone. Joy fizzed through her like a stream of bubbles.

"NEW YORK!" she said again, and Bill, not seeming to notice that Rose's life had been transformed by those two short words said, "Yes. Samantha and I are flying over very early tomorrow morning and I must say . . ."

"*NEW YORK TOMORROW MORNING!*" said Rose. "OH, DADDY! OH, DADDY! OH, DADDY!"

"Oh, *sweet*!" said Samantha. "Let's take her with us!"

"OH, YES! *TAKE* ME WITH YOU!" begged Rose, hands clasped, jumping up and down on a beautiful Chinese rug (in very grubby sandals), "OH DADDY, *PLEASE*! OH DADDY, *PLEASE, PLEASE*!"

"Really, Samantha, we did not need this!"

groaned Bill. "Rose darling, do you think you would like to take those sandals off? You could leave them by the door . . . Perhaps I should roll up the rugs . . ."

The jet stream of joyful bubbles was slowing down frighteningly quickly. Something was wrong. Some problem with her sandals?

"*Please* say you will take me to New York," she begged.

"Rose. Samantha was joking. Now take off those sandals."

It was the sandals.

"I am!" promised Rose, struggling with straps as she spoke. "I am taking them off!"

"Just *look* at your feet!"

Feet now.

Take them off? Not possible.

"Absolutely filthy, Rose!"

Filthy.

"I'll wash them!" said Rose anxiously.

"Good girl."

The bubbles began again. Rose rolled up the rug, handed it to her father, grabbed her sandals, arranged them by the door, and headed for the bathroom dizzy with relief.

"Bill, you never told me she was so little," whispered Samantha. "How could you bear to leave her?"

"I haven't left her!" snapped Bill. "I have always been there for her . . . Always! Oh, Rose! That was quick! Now, drink your orange juice and tell me about Caddy. I *will* take you to New York—"

"Daddy! Daddy!" cried Rose, and splashed down her orange juice as she rushed to hug him.

Bill pulled out a beautiful white handkerchief and hugged Rose with one hand while he mopped up orange juice with the other, "—but not *now*! When you are much older . . ."

"NO!" wailed Rose. "NO! NO!"

"Please stop making that horrible noise!"

"No, no, no!" sobbed Rose, thumping his chest as hard as she could with both fists together.

"Rose, I am losing patience here!"

"Please, Daddy, please!"

"Those are not real tears!"

Rose could no longer reply. The tears, real or not, had doubled her over. They battered her to her knees.

Samantha could not bear it. She put her arms around Rose and asked her, "Have you always wanted to go to New York, Rose sweetheart?"

"NO!" answered Bill, now quite sure whose side Samantha was on. "No, she has not! This is ridiculous! This is the first time the thought has crossed her mind! This is a tantrum! Nothing more!"

Rose knelt on the floor and sobbed onto the sofa (which fortunately was black leather and would wipe clean quite easily). Bill stamped out onto the balcony and peered vainly down the street, looking for Caddy. Samantha held on to Rose and murmured, "Hush, sweetheart, hush! Let me think!"

"Samantha, stop it!" shouted Bill in despair. "There is no question of Rose coming! She has no reason to come! She has no seat on the airplane! Besides . . ."

He paused, waiting for Samantha to look up. When she did, he shrugged his shoulders and mouthed, "Passport!"

That silenced Samantha, because she knew as well as anyone that nobody could travel anywhere without a passport. Unluckily for Bill she did not stay silent. She bent and explained to Rose, "Rose sweetheart, I should never have suggested it. You would need a passport . . ."

Somehow that word penetrated the misery

swamping Rose. Passport was not impossible. She made a wet blurry, lumpy sort of noise, like a person trying to talk under water. Only someone naturally excellent at understanding underwater speech could have possibly made any sense of it. Samantha was one of those rare people. She translated perfectly.

"Rose says she has her name on your passport, Bill!"

"She says what?"

"She says her name is on your passport."

"First I've heard of it," muttered Bill, looking incredibly shifty.

Rose made more of her noise.

"She says, 'Don't you remember?' When you had to get a new passport? And you had to put down her name? And you made a big fuss?"

"I made a big fuss?" asked Bill. "Me?"

This time Rose's noise was much more like human speech. She said quite plainly, between hiccups and huge sloshy sniffs, "Yes. You made a big fuss to Mummy because of my name. Because you hadn't seen my birth certificate till then. And you didn't know she really had called me Permanent Rose. So you had to put Permanent Rose on the passport. And you said what would people think. But you still put it on. Just in case. Like Caddy and Saffy and Indigo . . ."

"It had slipped my mind," said Bill stiffly.

"Please, Daddy, take me to New York and I will be good forever."

"No, Rose."

"Please."

Bill said that he was going into the street to look for Caddy, and marched out of the room. Samantha said, "Rose sweetheart. Stop crying. It's only making him crosser. Let's be sensible. Let me ring the airline and see if they've any seats. That's the first thing to do. And Rose . . ."

"Yes?" hiccuped Rose.

"Be nice to Bill while we wait for Caddy."

"I don't think it's any use waiting for Caddy."

"Be nice to him anyway. Please."

Rose nodded.

"Now go and wash your face in cool water while I phone."

The storm was over. Rose looked at Samantha with sudden hope. She seemed capable of anything.

Ten minutes later Rose was herself again. More than herself. Clean. Quiet. Sitting on the sofa, sitting on her hands, telling Samantha the news from home. Samantha had telephoned the airline and told her, "They're ringing back. That's the best I can do just now."

"Thank you."

"Tell me what you've all been doing this summer."

Rose said. "Nothing much. Mummy's been painting the hospital walls . . ."

"Mummy's been doing what?" asked Bill, coming in at that moment and sighing with relief at the transformation Samantha had managed in his absence.

"Painting the hospital walls," explained Rose as nicely as she could. "To cheer them up. She did pictures of rude statues for the old people and pictures of home for the children. It gets her out of the shed, Saffy and Sarah say."

"Eve hides from life in the garden shed," explained Bill to Samantha. "Doesn't she, Rose?"

"Yes," agreed Rose. "When she's not at the hospital. Or teaching at the college. Or doing her Young Offenders."

"I wouldn't call that list hiding from life," remarked Samantha to no one in particular.

"She goes to sleep there," Rose told her. "On an old pink sofa. And she paints pictures in there too. Only Daddy says they're not exactly Art . . ."

"Oh, does he?"

"Yes. But she hasn't done much painting this summer."

"Why not?"

"Too fed up," explained Rose devastatingly. "Because of . . ."

"Change the subject, Rose!" ordered Bill.

"When will the airplane people ring?"

"As soon as they can. I told them it's urgent."

"Rose," said Bill, "I want you to understand that you will not be coming with us to New York. For goodness' sake. And Samantha has only telephoned the airline to put your mind at rest (I presume) that there are no spare places on the plane. And why on earth do you want to go there anyway? I can think of no reason at all unless it is something to do with that American boy Indigo took up with. The one who was always getting into trouble . . ."

Inwardly Rose flinched, but outside she made no sign at all. She was concentrating on being nice. Also she knew that Samantha had not rung the airline to put her mind at rest that there were no seats. She had rung to try to get her a seat.

"Tell me about Indigo's olden days," suggested Samantha.

"They are in a book he has," said Rose. "It is called *Le Morte D'Arthur* and that means 'the death of Arthur.' The pages are all thin and yellowy gray and they stick to your fingers for too long when you try and turn them over. Indigo and me have been reading it all summer."

"And how much of it do you understand?" asked Bill.

"All of it. Lancelot and Arthur and Kay and all the others. They were friends," said Rose, and a stray, unaccountable tear rolled down one cheek.

It was a long, long afternoon. At intervals the telephone rang, never the airline, always friends of Bill, wanting to chat for hours. They waited for Caddy. They rang home, but there was no one to answer. Caddy was away. Eve was in the shed. Saffron was supervising Indigo shopping for clothes. ("It is about time you wore something that I could borrow now and then," she said, steering him into the Gap.

"That jacket. That top. Those and those. Hurry up!")

"Where can Caddy have got to?" moaned Bill for the hundredth time. "Why doesn't she answer her mobile?"

"It's switched off," said Rose.

"Why?"

"In case someone rings."

"What have I done?" moaned Bill, massaging his wrinkles in despair. "What have I done to deserve this?"

"Yes, what have you done?" asked Samantha.

Caddy still did not come. Samantha rang the airline again and was told she was number eleven in a queue. Bill cooked pasta. Rose, having described the rest of her family, launched into the subject of Saffron and Sarah, their terrible cooking, their cultivation of hearts of stone ("I'm with them there," said Samantha), and their search for Saffron's father.

The search for Saffron's father meant giving Samantha a quick family history, which Bill interrupted four times to say he did not think Samantha could possibly be interested.

"I am," said Samantha. "I am incredibly interested! You have never told me a word before! Go on, Rose. Where did Saffron look?"

Rose told her about the box of photographs and letters and diaries and notebooks that contained nothing at all.

"Nothing?" asked Samantha incredulously.

"No," said Rose. "Nothing. Did it, Daddy?"

"How would I know?" asked Bill, pacing the room like an animal in a cage.

"You packed it."

"Oh?"

"Mummy said."

"Well, when did Eve ever pack anything?"

"I can't believe *Eve* doesn't know," said Samantha.

"She would tell Saffy if she did," said Rose. "She said she would. She said that was fair."

"Who does Saffy look like?"

"Exactly like Caddy."

"Ah."

"And Caddy looks like Mummy."

"And Bill," said Samantha.

"What?"

"Nothing."

Bill stopped pacing and left the room. Samantha and Rose could hear him opening and closing drawers, slamming them shut one after another. Then the slamming stopped and he came in, gulping on a cigarette, and he said, "Time for bed, Rose!"

Rose stared at him in astonishment.

"Bill," said Samantha, "you don't seriously expect Rose to go to bed at half past five on a hot summer afternoon?"

"Yes, I do."

The phone in the hall rang again just then, luckily for Rose, who had been about to abandon being nice. Bill dashed off to answer it so fast he left a trail of blue smoke.

"He gave up smoking," said Rose.

"I know." Samantha nodded, and they both looked curiously at Bill, who saw them looking and turned his back.

"It's true," said Rose. "Caddy does look a bit like him, too. I never noticed before. What if that's the airplane people on the phone?"

"It isn't; Bill would have told us."

Bill finished talking and came back, lit another cigarette, and asked, "Packing all done, Samantha darling?"

"Yes."

"You always forget something."

"No I don't."

"Better check."

"I'm talking to Rose."

"So I see. I'll try ringing Eve again."

"Where else did Saffron look for her father?" questioned Samantha.

"On the Internet," said Rose.

Bill, who had just gone out of the room, nearly fell back in again.

"On the Internet?" he demanded. "And what did she think she would find on the Internet, for heaven's sake?"

"People do look for people on the Internet," said Rose. "I've just remembered why no one is at home. It's Sarah's mother's birthday party. They're having a barbecue and we were all invited. Probably no one will be back for ages."

"Sweet angels of mercy, lead me away!" moaned Bill, and he banged his head three times on the wall on purpose.

"You were telling us about Saffy looking for her father on the Internet," said Samantha, who seemed very determined to get to the end of the story. "Go on!"

Bill stopped banging his head and lit himself two more cigarettes, one to smoke and one to cradle in his hands. He had to keep changing them over to make sure that neither of them went out.

"Symbolic," said Samantha, glaring at him.

Nobody seemed to hear her at first. Bill did not even look up. Rose was in a dream where she arrived in New York and saw Tom standing under a sign that read NEW YORK.

"So, what did Saffron find on the Internet?" asked Samantha.

Rose dragged herself away from New York and thought backward to Sarah's house. The laughter she had heard outside the bedroom, and the cardboard heroes that kept falling over. The computer screen burning in the warm summer gloom because the curtains had been drawn to shut out the glare. An unfathomable picture of a hat and a carton of milk. 'Bill Casson, Seriously Now.' It all seemed very long ago.

"She found Daddy," said Rose at last.

Chapter Eleven

SARAH'S MOTHER'S PARTY WAS NEARLY OVER. THE CANDLES on the packet-mix birthday cake had been blown out, and the cake had been cut up and handed out by Sarah to anyone she could persuade to eat it. At Sarah's third attempt at cake making she had dispensed with all fancy recipes. She had concentrated her efforts entirely on largeness, iced it pink, and sprinkled jelly beans among the forty-five candles.

"Make a wish," she ordered, as she dealt the gluey slabs to her victims.

Most people wished they hadn't agreed to sample the birthday cake.

Not everyone, though.

Indigo looked up at the summer stars and remembered the evening he and Tom had spent renaming them, just before Tom left. He wished he knew where Tom was now.

• • •

Saffron came across to Sarah's table, looked very dubiously at the cake, and said, "Admit it is not one of your finest creations!"

"It is hideous," said Sarah cheerfully, "and the jelly beans are from a packet I had at Christmas, and it is now September. I am only slightly hopeful that it is not poisonous. What! You are not going to eat it, are you, Saffy? Good grief, you must be mad!"

"Shut up and let me concentrate," ordered Saffron. "I am making my wish!"

"Well, you be careful what you wish for!"

"I will."

Saffron thought briefly of her unknown father, and then at much more length of the eleventh-grade boy at school who did the music for the discos. She wished that he would ask her out without her having to make him.

Sarah's mother wished she would not get any older, and then hastily unwished it, realizing that the alternative was worse.

Eve wished everyone would live happily ever after.

• • •

David had arrived at the Casson house much earlier that afternoon. He seemed to be unable to stop telling Rose's family how sorry he was to have accidentally dispatched Rose to London. He was so apologetic that even Saffron said, "Relax, David! Caddy telephoned and said she had her safe."

"I still don't know why she had to go tearing after Caddy in the first place," said Indigo.

"There was something she had to give to her," explained David.

"What?"

"I promised I wouldn't tell."

"Well," said Eve. "She will be company for Caddy, so that's good, but I shall be glad to have her home again. The house already feels empty without her."

"It does," agreed Saffron. "Nothing left but the dirty handprints and the pictures on the walls."

They all looked mournfully at the pictures on the walls. Even the one of Tom as Sir Lancelot under a sign that read NEW YORK struck no one as funny. David said, for about the twelfth time, that he hoped she was okay.

He followed Saffy and Indigo throughout the day,

repeating this remark, and when everyone went off to Sarah's house, David tagged along too. He got into the party spirit straight away. Seeing Indigo being greeted with a hug by Sarah's mother, he bravely joined in by kissing Sarah herself, loudly and clumsily on her left ear.

This was a bit of a shock to Sarah's father, who took his daughter aside at once. "I promised you when you were born that I would never criticize your boyfriends," he said. "So do not be afraid to introduce me, Sarah. I will not disgrace you by weeping in public, but I may get slightly drunk."

"It's all right," Sarah reassured him. "He is not my sort at all (short hair and politeness will never appeal to me). He is someone Indigo knows and is too kind to shoo away. His name is David."

Sarah's father, although not at all reassured by this information, said in that case he was more than welcome, obviously worse was to come, and he looked forward to meeting the long-haired yob who would eventually claim his daughter's heart. Soon David was helping with the barbecue as if he were one of the family. He seemed very at home. (Later, when the photographs of the evening were eventually developed, he was discovered to be in nearly all of them.)

"I hope you're not going to kiss me again," said Sarah when David came ambling across for his birthday cake. "It is too scary for my poor father (not to mention me). I saw you posing with my mother under the Happy Birthday banner! I didn't know you even knew her!"

"No, I don't," said David with his mouth full of cake.

"I expect that's why you didn't bring her a present?"

"Yes," agreed David.

"What do you think of the cake?"

"Fantastic."

"I made it."

"I know."

"You gobbled that bit so quickly I don't suppose you had time to make a wish."

"I did," said David. "I wished Rose would be okay."

Sarah looked at him more favorably than she ever had done before and said, "Take another slice."

"All right," said David, helping himself.

"Then you can make another wish."

David nodded, chewing.

"So what was it?"

"Oh," said David, surprised. "I wished Rose would be okay again."

"Have some more," suggested Sarah, and when he had taken another piece and eaten it, she asked, "Did you wish about Rose again?"

"Yes," said David, wiping cake crumbs up from his plate and sucking them off his fingers. "Just that she would be okay."

"Isn't there anything you want for yourself?"

David thought about that and eventually replied that he shouldn't mind a set of drums. Sarah offered the plate again.

"Thanks," said David, eating only slightly more slowly.

With his next piece (prompted by Sarah), he wished his old wish to be thin and swift and witty and effortlessly cool, and with his sixth piece he wished for drumming lessons to go with the drums, but all the time, at the back of these wishes, he was wishing for Rose to be okay.

He shook his head speechlessly at the offer of a seventh piece of cake.

"Rose will be okay," said Sarah kindly.

• • •

Then the party was over. The barbecue was cold. The music was quiet. Helpful people wandered around with black garbage bags, filling them with paper plates, napkins, plastic glasses, and candle stumps. Eve, who had drunk a great deal of wine, had a particularly heavy bag because she had also inadvertently tidied away two cameras, several small birthday presents, and the barbecue tools. (Luckily her bag split before these things were lost for good.)

"Bed," she said, hugging Sarah's mother good-bye. "Lovely party! Off we go! Where's Saffy?"

"I'm stopping the night with Sarah," said Saffron.

"Oh, yes. Indy?"

"Here," said Indigo.

"MarcusJoshPatrick?"

"I'm here too," said David.

"Rose?" asked Eve, stopping suddenly, halfway along the road to home.

"London, with Caddy."

"I knew that."

At the door of the house she asked, "Bill?"

"Looking after Rose," said Indigo soothingly.

"Darling Bill. Bed or shed? Which is nearer?"

"About the same," said Indigo.

"Shed, I think," said Eve. "No stairs. Night, night darlings!"

Eve hovered for a moment, and then set off down the garden path. David watched her with his mouth hanging open.

"It's a very comfortable shed," said Indigo. "It's got a sofa and quilts and cushions and stuff."

"Crikey."

The shed door creaked, then closed. And then there was a new sound. It came from inside the house. It was the telephone ringing, and as soon as Indigo and David heard it, they both exclaimed, "Rose!"

While Sarah's mother's birthday party had been just getting underway, in London the last of the sunlight was shining low through the sliding glass doors of Bill Casson's apartment. It showed up a pattern of handprints on the glass, low down and small-size, clustered together like a constellation.

Mine, thought Rose, recognizing them in surprise. *I don't remember putting my hands there. I did look outside, though. Daddy will say, "Rose,* look *at those marks on the glass!" He hates mess. You can tell when you look at this room that he really hates mess. You could not be cozy in this room. You could not lie down on the floor and draw. You could play a guitar because you can play a guitar anywhere. Tom can play his lying down flat on his back. He crosses one leg over to make a place to rest it . . .*

"Rose!" said Samantha, interrupting Rose's thoughts. "Say that again! About what Saffron found when she was looking for her father on the Internet."

"Oh," said Rose innocently, not really concentrating, still much more interested in her own thoughts. "Oh, yes. She found Daddy."

Bill flung himself up from the sofa, dragged open the balcony doors, and stepped into the sudden noise of traffic and the warm dusty air of a London evening. He only stayed outside for a moment. Then he came back in and pulled the doors shut again. Rose saw that Samantha was staring at him as if the person who had stepped back in was a completely different individual from the one who had gone out a minute before.

Samantha said, "Saffron found you! You! Now I understand everything."

Rose thought, *Now he has made fingerprints on the glass too. Good.*

Bill said, "How am I ever going to face them again? Saffron? Eve?" And he sat on the sofa with his head in his hands, holding it like it was a ball he had just caught before it fell.

Samantha asked, "Do you really think that Eve does not know you are Saffron's father?"

Then, for the first time, Rose understood everything too.

Rose was still not yet nine. The facts of life were recent news to her. She had heard them first at school (in inaccurate, alarming, and completely unbelievable detail). Then she had tested her new knowledge on Saffron and Sarah and been told them again.

"For a start," Sarah had said, "they are not *all* of the facts of life! Knowing them does not mean you know everything (some people think it does). They are *some* of the facts of life. You shouldn't listen to mucky little boys in the playground, Rosy Pose!"

"I *had* to listen!"

The information Rose heard from Saffron and Sarah was much less alarming (and sometimes hilarious) and much more accurate, but equally unbelievable. At the end she had asked, "Is it truly not all a big joke?"

"It's a big joke," Saffron had told her. "But it's true."

"For some people?"

"For everyone."

"Except me," said Rose.

"Just what I said when I first heard it all," remarked Sarah cheerfully.

"It can be true for everyone except me!" said Rose. "And all the people I know!"

Saffron said, "Oh, all right then, Rosy Pose! It can be that way if you like."

Now, incredibly, it seemed that it could not be that way if Rose liked. Bill was saying, very slowly, one word dropping at a time, "I . . . don't . . . know . . ."

Rose's whole world had gone spinning up into the air, like a penny flipped high, turning and turning.

". . . if . . . Eve . . . knows . . ."

Higher and higher, until it seemed that everything she had believed in must be spilled and scattered and lost.

". . . I . . . am . . . Saffron's . . . father."

Coming down again.

"But . . . it's . . . true."

And landing, right side up.

Rose gave a huge sigh of relief because it was all still there. Saffron. Sarah. Caddy. Michael. Indigo. Eve. Tom. All still there. And even Bill. The world had spun, and risen upward, and tumbled back down again, and they had survived the flight. And so had she.

Nevertheless, she was hugely astonished.

She said, "Daddy! You are Saffy's father! You! Goodness! No wonder! No wonder Saffy looks just like Caddy! No wonder there was nothing in the box! What an enormous, ENORMOUS secret to keep for so long!"

"Yes," said Bill. "What an enormous secret to keep for so long."

He looked so unhappy, so unlike his usual arrogant, charming, confident self, that Rose was sorry for him.

"New York will cheer you up," she told him consolingly.

Bill lifted his head a little.

"Aren't you angry with me, Rose?"

"What, me?" asked Rose, surprised, and Samantha suddenly crossed the room, dropped a kiss on the top of her head, and went out, closing the door.

"Yes, you."

"Why? Because you're Saffy's father or because you don't want to take me to New York?"

"Rose, could we just drop the subject of New York?"

"All right. No. I'm not angry."

"Sad?"

"Because you are Saffy's father?"

"Yes."

Rose shook her head. "No."

"Thank you, Rose."

"I am sad because you don't want to take me to New York though."

Bill sighed.

"And I think Saffy will be angry."

"Yes."

"And Caddy and Indigo might say, 'A bit sneaky.' Being Saffy's father and not telling anyone. Because they will know what you must have done to be Saffy's father."

"I suppose they will."

"They know the facts of life. And they believe them too. So."

"And I suppose you know them as well, Rosy Pose?"

"Yes," said Rose, cheerfully. "But don't worry. I don't believe them."

"Oh, Rose."

"And if the others say, 'A bit sneaky,' and are very mad, I will be on your side until they calm down."

Bill lifted his head right up. He took his hands away and it stayed balanced on his neck where it had always been. He said, "Darling, brave, loyal Rose. No wonder your mother called you Permanent Rose."

"Can we talk about New York now?" asked Rose hopefully.

"Rose!" exclaimed Indigo and David when they heard the telephone ring, and they dashed into the house and grabbed it, and they were right; it was Rose.

"Is she okay?" demanded David, crowding up close to the receiver so that he could hear too. "Ask her if she's okay!"

"Are you okay, Rose?" asked Indigo. "Where are you? Is Caddy there too? Why are you calling so late?"

"Because you weren't in earlier," said Rose. "We tried and tried. Me and Daddy."

"Is that where you are?"

"Of course it is! He's asleep on the sofa right now.

He's got stress because Samantha dumped him (tell Mummy, she'll be pleased). Caddy's lost."

"What do you mean, 'lost'?"

"She rushed away and didn't come back. But it doesn't matter. I shan't be on my own. Daddy said I can go with him."

"Go with him? *Where?*"

"And Samantha, who is very nice, bought me a lot of new clothes from Tescos because it stays open so late. Jeans and pajamas and two T-shirts in a pack, and a blue skirt and a bag with a toothbrush shaped like a dinosaur . . ."

"Stop a minute, Rose!" begged Indigo.

Rose stopped for a moment, but she had never had so many new things all at once in her life before, and the wonder had not yet left her. She stopped, but she started again almost immediately.

"And a sponge shaped like a dinosaur to match the toothbrush. And socks and underwear (not dinosaur, just normal) and three pairs of sneakers, because she didn't know what size would fit me. You should have seen it; it was amazing, she just walked in with three big bags and said, 'There you are, Rose.' And they were all full of things for me.

And all the sneakers fit if I scrunch my toes up a bit in the smallest and walk slowly in the biggest so they don't fall off, but I am taking the middle-size pair . . ."

"Taking the middle-size pair *where*?" shouted Indigo.

"On the plane, and I forgot to say a sweatshirt with a hood, because Samantha said it might be cold. Even if it's hot here and hot there, it might be cold in the sky in between. Samantha says."

"What sky in between?" asked Indigo, although he was beginning to guess.

"London and New York."

"Rose!"

"Daddy said he would take me if there was a seat on the plane and if Mummy said yes. And there was a seat on the plane. Samantha's. So."

"Rose, do you think you are going to find Tom in New York?"

"Of course I am," said Rose.

"How?" demanded Indigo. "And anyway, what about Mum saying yes? She hasn't!"

"She will. And of course I will find Tom in New York. It's where he lives."

"Rose," said Indigo, "what do you think is going to happen? Do you think you will land and find Tom standing under a sign that says 'New York'? I think you ought to talk to Mum. Speak to David while I go and fetch her!"

Indigo passed the receiver over to David and hurried outside. David said, "Hello, Rose."

"Why are you at our house in the middle of the night?"

"I just am. Are you okay?"

"Of course I'm okay," said Rose. "At eight o'clock tomorrow morning guess where I will be?"

"Where?"

"In the sky!"

"Only if your mum says yes."

"Mummy always says yes," said Rose truthfully. "And Daddy has done already. He's even put a label on my bag, so that proves it! 'Heathrow, London, to JFK, New York.' I keep reading it."

"Well, I think your mum will say no."

"Why?"

"Mine would."

"Oh," said Rose. "David?"

"Yes?"

"If she says no, I won't be able to go."

"Why doesn't your father talk to her?"

"He said he couldn't face it. Because of why Samantha dumped him. David?"

"Yes?"

"I've got a good idea. Tell Mummy to telephone if it's no. And if she doesn't, we will know it's yes and I can go to New York . . ."

"I can't do that! Anyway, here she is coming . . ."

". . . Because I really have to go to New York," said Rose, "and I've got to go now because I have to go to bed."

And she put down the receiver, inspected the base of her father's telephone, muted the ringer, found the answering machine button, and turned that off too. To make extra sure that she was safe, she picked up her father's mobile from where it was lying on the coffee table and switched that off as well.

Then she shook Bill awake and said, "I rang home and I can go!"

"That's good, Rosy Pose," said Bill very sleepily and now long past all battles. "So Eve said yes. I suppose she would say yes."

"She said yes," said Rose. "The way people do when they don't say no."

"She didn't say no, did she?"

"No."

"All right, Rosy Pose."

After Caddy had abandoned Rose, she recrossed London, caught the next train home, and rushed straight to Michael's house. Hours later, when she came away, she left Michael with the diamond and platinum ring.

"At least I didn't get it engraved," said Michael. "I'll find some other girl to give it to, and she'll never know that it wasn't hers from the start."

"Oh Michael, don't joke!" wailed Caddy.

"What else am I supposed to do?" demanded Michael. "What else am I supposed to do when I feel like this? Cadmium darling."

It was two o'clock in the morning before Caddy got home. She unlocked the door, tiptoed up the stairs, and crawled into bed. Her last thought, before she fell asleep, was that she had had enough of the world for one day.

• • •

Indigo had fallen asleep thinking about Rose and Tom. He dreamed that his hands were tied. He fought against the wrappings. They were thin and fragile, but there were hundreds of them. As fast as he could tear them away, more and more came and folded around him.

In the morning the pages of *Le Morte D'Arthur* were scattered as thick as fallen leaves in a forest, all over the bed and floor.

Eve dreamed she was an infinitely small dot, rocking in an infinitely large darkness. It was her favorite dream.

Saffron said she dreamed of nothing.

"Nothing?" asked Sarah. "That's not possible! I dreamed of that eleventh-grade boy who does the school discos. . . ."

Saffron flounced out of bed.

". . . He was . . . Saffy, you pig! Take those things off lovely Justin!"

"No," said Saffy, getting back into bed and looking

at lovely Justin (dressed for the day in a fringed denim skirt and blue lace bra). "They fit him perfectly. That'll teach you to dream."

Saffy and Sarah's hearts of stone were never very solid first thing in the morning.

Caddy woke up and exclaimed, "Rose!" She had forgotten all about Rose.

All through the night Bill, sleeping on the sofa, was sure that he was a picture. A picture in a gallery, slipping slowly down the wall. "Oh, really!" complained Bill, as he slid. "I am not exactly . . ."

Then he woke up and found himself on the floor, and remembered that this was the day he was taking Rose to New York. Rose, not Samantha.

I have no choice, thought Bill. *What else could I do? Let her go home? Now that she knows about Saffron?*

He went across the hall to look at Rose, asleep in his bed. The clothes that Samantha had bought her were laid in loving piles around the pillows. The new sneakers made lumps under the quilt.

The dinosaur sponge was hugged under her chin, like a teddy bear. She looked so completely content that it was a shame to wake her up, but even as he looked at her, she opened her eyes and asked, "Is it time to go?"

"Yes," said Bill. "Nearly. Nearly time to go."

Chapter Twelve

ROSE THOUGHT, I NEVER GUESSED ON MONDAY MORNING THAT *on Friday morning I would be sitting on an airplane ready to fly to Tom-in-New-York. I never guessed it on Tuesday morning either. Or Wednesday. Or Thursday.*

The plane had just begun to move. Rose was trying very hard not to be frightened.

She had a seat with a window, a small rectangle hardly bigger than her face. Through it she watched the airport buildings become smaller as the plane chugged (at the speed of an old town bus) to the end of the runway. She could not imagine how they would ever fly.

Then the tremendous acceleration began. Her ears hurt and an enormous force pushed her into the back of her seat. Beyond the window the ground tilted away, the earth turned sideways, and the window filled with a blur of dingy colored patchwork, menacingly close.

Fear washed over Rose like a great cold wave. She cried, "Daddy!" as she went under, and from somewhere as far away as another world she felt him take her hand.

"All right, Rosy Pose?" said Bill.

Rose could only gasp.

"Open your eyes."

Rose opened her eyes. Amazing. Blue sky outside, and the earth back where it should be, far, far below. For a minute Rose had thought it was going to come charging in through the window.

"Perfectly safe," said Bill, but he still held her small cold hand firmly in his warm, brown one. "Remember how the planes look, crossing the sky?"

Rose nodded.

"All those jet-trail white lines?"

"Yes."

"Thousands of people fly all over the world every day."

"I know," said Rose, and she thought, *Tom did. Just like this.*

"Are we making a white line right now?" she asked.

"I expect so."

Rose wished she could see it: her own line drawn across the sky. Her biggest picture ever, an immense white stroke sweeping across a clear blue background. Only God drew bigger pictures than airplanes. She imagined him (surely at this height not far overhead) stooping down to admire her work, wondering how it would end.

Silently, in her head, she commanded God, "Step over it! It's not finished yet!"

It will end with Tom, Rose thought.

Friday morning at the Casson house was not good. Saffron and Sarah came home to a tremendous fuss. Nobody was dressed and everybody was talking at once. Too many things had to be explained: the sudden reappearance of Caddy (who was supposed to be looking after Rose in London), the dumping of Michael, and the exit of Samantha. Worst of all, the fact that even now Rose was on an eight o'clock flight from Heathrow in London to JFK airport in New York, in the confident belief that she would find Tom there waiting for her.

"I should never have stayed at Sarah's!" said Saffy. "If I'd spoken to Rose, I would not have let her go! Fancy giving the phone to that dope David, Indigo! You know it was David who sent her off after Caddy in the first place!"

"I should never have left her in London!" moaned Caddy. "All I could think of was Michael . . ."

"I can't believe you've dumped Michael!" said Indigo as he headed to the shower.

"Neither can I!" said Caddy, and started crying again.

Only Eve was in any way happy. She knew she should not be, but she could not help it. The news of Samantha made her feel much less of a single mother. Nor was she as disturbed as the rest at the thought of Rose's desolate, Tom-less arrival in New York. Like Rose, she could not imagine such a possibility. She said, "Bill will take care of Rose. Darling Bill! Saffy, I don't think it would have made any difference if you had been here; Rose would still have gone . . . Is that the door? Yes, it is! It's that boy MarcusJoshPatrick! And Indy is in the shower and nobody is dressed except Saffron and Sarah, and he always stays for ages! Saffy darling, do you think you could go down and very kindly and tactfully get rid of him?"

Saffron gave a great groan.

“I’ll go!” offered Sarah, scrambling to her feet and setting off with her wobbly mermaid walk to the top of the stairs. “I’m brilliant at getting rid of people; I do it all the time at home!” (She tobogganed swiftly down the stairs on her bottom.) “Just wait and see!”

A minute later she had crossed the kitchen, pulled open the door, hooked it closed behind her, and toppled forward into David’s arms, causing him to take several steps backward and temporarily forget everything that had ever happened to him in the preceding thirteen years.

“Crikey!” said David, clutching Sarah as if she were an unexpected gift from the gods, dropped down from the sky. “Crikey, I never . . . I didn’t know you . . . Is this nearly like snogging? No, no! I never said that!”

“Yes, you did, and no, it isn’t,” said Sarah, unwrapping herself from his arms. “Nothing like snogging, as I am sure you will one day discover (although not with me). You can let go now. I will not fall over. Now then, why are you here?”

“I came to see what was happening,” said David. “I couldn’t stop thinking about Rose and wondering if she was okay. So I thought I’d come around early and see.”

"So did I," said Sarah. "But it's no good. I was glad to get out (you were a perfect excuse, David). They are not dressed and seriously stressed and things are not happy. They don't want visitors. What were you thinking of, zooming Rose away to London like that, and then letting her take off for New York?"

"She said she was going to find Tom."

"She won't find Tom. That's mostly what they are all so upset about in there." Sarah nodded toward the closed door. "Come on, we'll go to my house. Saffron left my chair outside. You can help push if you like (you don't know how you are honored). David, think of Rose arriving in New York, and no Tom!"

"Well, he doesn't know she's coming, does he?" asked David, feeling very self-conscious as he steered Sarah out onto the street. "He'd be there if he knew."

"Do you think so?"

"He'd go to the airport. Are you sure it's all right, me doing this? Pushing you?"

"Of course it is!"

"I feel like a girl-burglar!"

Sarah laughed, then asked, "Do you really think Tom would go and meet Rose if he knew? Saffy and I thought he'd just gone back home and forgotten everyone. No one's heard a word since he went."

David thought about this all the way to Sarah's front gate. Then he said, "Tom's not heard from no one then neither."

"No," agreed Sarah, after translating this observation into English in her head.

"Someone ought to tell him about Rose."

"How? No one knows where he is."

"Someone must."

"Not here. He never told anyone. Not Indigo and Rose. Not the people at the music shop. And the house where he stayed is empty. His grandmother has gone too."

"Doesn't anyone know where she's gone either?"

"No. Indigo asked the neighbors, and all they knew was America. And he asked the postman, and he said he couldn't tell him even if he knew. Confidential. Do you want to come inside or stop in the garden?"

"Stop in the garden," said David, parking Sarah by the picnic table. "I like your garden. It looked nice last night with the lights."

"Yes."

"And it looks nice now as well, with the rubbish picked up . . . Sarah, who knows where you live?"

“What?” asked Sarah, surprised.

“Who’d have it written down?”

“Oh, I see what you mean! Loads of people. I’d be easy to track down. Family. Friends. The hospital. The swimming pool because I have a season ticket. The library. Drama club. Every time you join something you have to give an address! But I don’t think Tom joined things when he was here. Who would know where you live, David, if they wanted to track you down?”

David thought and thought. Who did? His mum. His granddad. He had never been in the hospital, and he didn’t join things any more than Tom had done.

“The police would be able to track me down,” he said regretfully. “From when I got a Caution. But that’s no help because Tom never got in trouble with the police. He got in trouble at school though . . .”

“School!” exclaimed Sarah. “School! You are right! They will have his address! Why didn’t we think of school! Come on!”

“But it’s still the holidays!”

“If you think schools are shut all through the holidays you are wrong,” said Sarah. “My mother is at her school right now, getting ready for next term.

School will be open! The secretary will be there! They will have Tom's address! They keep stuff like that for years and years! Brilliant, clever you! Don't just stand there! Get off to school and get it!"

"How?"

"Ask."

"Go to school and ask for Tom's address?"

"Yes, of course! Quickly! And then come back here! Oh, I wish I could run!"

The frustration in Sarah's voice when she said that was what finally set David running. He ran for five minutes. Then he turned around and ran back. Sarah was still where he had left her, her hands gripped together as if she were praying. She looked horrified to see him return so soon. She wailed, "Oh, why have you come back?"

"I had to. They'd never tell me Tom's address."

"You didn't even try!"

"Because I know! That secretary doesn't like me. She thinks I'm rubbish. I've took stuff from that office. She caught me at it once. I bet she remembers!"

"Of course she won't!"

"So I came back for you," said David. "I bet she likes you!" And before Sarah could reply, he had seized the handles of her wheelchair and begun pushing her to school.

"David pushed you all the way to school?" asked Saffron when Sarah reached this point in her narration of the events of that morning.

"Yes."

"You made him."

"No I didn't. And that's nothing to what he did next."

When they arrived at school at last, David saw that Sarah had been right. It was open. Strangely clean, strangely silent, strangely empty, but open. There were people about—voices in the staff room, the caretaker at the door (ignoring David, whom he always said was trouble) smiling at Sarah and saying, "Couldn't you wait till Monday then, madam? I've had a new grandson since I saw you last, and one of these days I will bring him in and you can see what a champion he is!"

Nobody, thought David, ever talked to him like that, and if they had, he would not have known how to answer as Sarah did, inserting the right replies at the right moments: "That's right, I couldn't wait. . . .

Oh, a new baby! What's he called? . . . Oliver? Oliver is my favorite name! You've got to bring him in; everyone will want to see him! I could give him a ride in my chair, and we will get him a present: I will do a collection as soon as we are back! I saw tiny, weeny newborn-baby-size soccer shoes in a shop in town; they would be perfect! Come on, David! We'll just rush in, and then when we come out, you can have thought whether shoes would be all right. Soft shoes, of course. No studs. *Come on,* David!"

Then, after all that thinking and hoping and running and talking, there was no one in the office. Sarah knocked and called, "Mrs. Smith, it's only me! Sarah! Hullo! Anyone in?" and then said, "Perhaps she's on the phone," and pushed open the door and said, "Mrs. Smith? Oh! Oh look, David!"

There was a note on the secretary's desk:

TO ALL STAFF!

MRS. SMITH WILL BE IN FROM 2–3:30 P.M.

ONLY UNTIL TERM RECOMMENCES.

"Bother!" said Sarah. "We cannot possibly wait until two o'clock! If Rose left early this morning, she will be nearly in New York by then! Let's try the staff room!"

On the staff room door was another notice:

MEETING IN PROGRESS

"Let's go back to the caretaker," said Sarah. "Maybe he could help."

But the caretaker had wandered off to talk to his daughter on his mobile about soccer shoes for the baby.

"Well," said Sarah. "There's nothing else for it. We will have to crash the staff meeting. I hope you are feeling brave!"

There was no reply. She looked around, and discovered she was suddenly alone.

"David!" she called crossly, and when there was no reply, she called again.

"Shut up!"

He was back again, tugging urgently at her chair.

"We'll have to go into the staff room," she told him.

"No, we won't! Why won't this thing go?"

"Brake! Hey! What are you doing?"

"Running," said David, running.

"But what about . . ."

"Shut up!"

"David!"

"Shut up, *please*!" begged David, already halfway down the drive.

"David, what about your brilliant idea? I promise I'll do all the talking . . . David, stop!"

David ran faster, right out of the school grounds and down the road.

"Stop, or I'll scream for help!"

"All right."

David crossed two pedestrian crossings, turned a corner, wiped the sweat from his forehead with the front of his T-shirt, carried on another few hundred yards to be on the safe side, parked Sarah beside a garbage can, and leaned over the handles of the wheelchair, wheezing and grunting.

"David! What ever is the matter?"

"Heck, that was scary," said David, sounding exactly like his granddad, and then he began rooting about down the front of his jeans.

"David! Stop it! That is totally gross . . . Good grief!"

David produced a sheet of paper. A form. Green.

With a heading: Student Information (Confidential). And subheadings: Name, DOB, Nationality, Contact telephone numbers, Addresses (at least two to be provided, Relationship to Student, parent/guardian/other), Any known medical problems, Allergies (nb asthma sufferers please see section on reverse of form), Other relevant information . . .

David did not allow Sarah to read very much. He merely pointed to the first subheading: "Name: Thomas Levin."

"Nicked it out the office," said David, and he stuffed it back down his jeans and started running again, and this time Sarah did not complain. In fact, she tried to make herself lighter. *Streamlined,* she thought, and held on tight and faced bravely into the wind.

Nicked it! she marveled as they sped along. *What a hero! How brave! How cool! How totally the right thing to do!*

David did not stop running (if it could be called running, more of a sodden gallop really, and if he had not had the wheelchair to hold on to, he would certainly have fallen over) until they were back at Sarah's house.

• • •

"I thought stealing it would be quickest," he explained, collapsing down at the picnic table, as limp and soaked and exhausted as a person pulled from a bog. "I knew where they were in that big filing cabinet. Saw them put mine in there the time I had to have a new one when we moved houses. It's got his phone number on it and everything. In New York. As well as his gran's here. It's got where he lives. Everything."

Then Sarah said, "You nicked it! What a hero! How brave! How cool! How totally the right thing to do!"

David knew then, just for a moment, what it felt like to be giddy with happiness.

"So, go in and telephone right now!" said Sarah, bringing him down.

"What, me?" asked David, aghast.

"There's a phone in my mum's office and I will guard the door, but actually there is no one in except Mrs. Silver, who cleans."

"What, me?" said David again. "*Me* telephone Tom in New York?"

"And explain that Rose is on her way right now and will be at the airport in four and a half hours' time. (It's a seven-hour flight, Caddy looked it up.)"

"Me!"

"And he must be there. Somehow. He must, because poor little Rose if he isn't. But he will be when he knows. You said so yourself! Come on! I'll show you the phone!"

"Why me?"

"Gosh, David," said Sarah, astonished as she led him inside. "Didn't you work out how to find him? And go and steal his address! And run all the way back with it, pushing me? (You must have lost pounds!) You are a hero! Just like in Indigo's book. Here's the telephone . . . Sit down . . . That's right! Aren't you the knight in shining armor, charging to the rescue? Of course you are!" said Sarah, giving him a hug. "There! Dial! Good grief, it's ringing, it's ringing! I can't bear it, I'm not as brave as you. I'll be right outside!"

"Hello, hello," she heard him say from the other side of the door. "It's someone called David from England . . . David . . . Yes, for Tom. It's important. Did I wake up the baby? I'm sorry. If you told Tom it was about Rose . . . Yes. Rose . . . Hello, Tom?"

That was how David (of all shining heroes, of all gallant knights, the most unlikely) managed to find

Tom again for Rose. Just as he had imagined doing once before, in the hot empty garden with the lost ring, and the dead cat, where he had found her searching for Tom. And also, just as he had imagined, when the quest was achieved, when Tom was produced (with as much of a flourish as he could manage from three and a half thousand miles away), Rose did not give one thought to David.

She did not think of anyone except Tom. Because there he was, as she had always known that he would be. Standing (as instructed by David) under a sign that read NEW YORK. Smiling and waving.

"Hello, Tom!" she cried, running up to him, and Tom said, as he sometimes did when he was very pleased to see her, "Hello, Permanent Rose!"

Chapter Thirteen

"SO, WHY?" ASKED SAFFRON AND SARAH WHEN ROSE WAS AT last home again, grubby, jet-lagged, triumphant, and laden with terrible presents ("Just the sort Daddy brings back," said Rose, handing out Empire State Building snow globes, baseball caps, stars and stripes T-shirts, and light-up Statues of Liberty that played "The Star-Spangled Banner"). "Why did he never write? Telephone? Send us a messenger pigeon? Contact us in any way? Callous beyond belief or callous beyond belief? Probably which?"

"He did ring," said Rose. "Twice."

"He didn't!"

"He did, and I heard him. Right at the beginning of the summer. But nobody else heard, and I thought it was a dream. Don't you remember?"

They did then, vaguely, remember hearing Eve and Rose talk of something like that.

"But why didn't he keep on telephoning?" asked Saffron.

"Because we didn't," said Rose.

"How could we have?"

"He didn't think, How could we have. He just thought we didn't."

"The dope!" exclaimed Sarah, and Indigo and Rose, who liked dopes, smiled at each other.

"At first they were all terribly worried about Frances," explained Rose. "Frances, his sister (She's learned my name, only she says 'Wose.' She shouts, 'WOSE!' She's really funny). They thought she was going to die. She took ages to get well. And Tom thought we were horrible, not even asking how Frances was or anything. Especially when he'd given Indigo his guitar . . . Poor Tom!"

"Poor Tom!" repeated Sarah scornfully and sarcastically. "How sad!"

"It was sad for him," insisted Rose. "It is sad when you think your friends don't care. It is, isn't it, Indy?"

"Yep," said Indigo.

"So he was very fed up with us," went on Rose. "And he gave up on us. He sulked. His grandmother told me (she's staying there with them, but she'll be home again soon) that he sulked all summer! He's a very good sulker," said Rose admiringly. "He sulked until David telephoned and got them all out of bed at six o'clock in the morning. . . ."

"I did not!" said David, indignantly. "It was nearly lunchtime that day I telephoned! Not six o'clock! Nothing like!"

"It was six o'clock in New York," said Rose.

David gave her a look of affectionate disbelief and for about the tenth time that day took off and admired the baseball cap she had brought him. ("I needed a hat," he had said, overwhelmed with pleasure when she gave it to him.) David's baseball cap had a big red apple on the front that flashed if it was banged very hard. Caddy had a similar one, only instead of an apple it said I LOVE NY with a pulsating, flashing heart for the *love.*

"To remind you of Michael," said Rose.

Michael was gone now. Quite suddenly. He had given up being a driving instructor, bought himself a leather jacket and pants and a secondhand motorbike ("He must have sold your ring," said Saffron callously), and disappeared into the sunset with Luke. After that, the only proof anyone had that he had not forgotten them was by way of Rose. The Early Morning Rose Delivery Service (bringing roses to Roses) did not stop. From all around the edge of Europe, Michael sent postcards to Rose, and all of them pictures of roses. This drove Caddy wild. She came home from college every weekend to inspect the postmark on the latest card, and she pinned a map of Europe to her bedroom wall and began to mark the progress of his journey with little silver flags.

"You could fly over," suggested Saffron and Sarah, "and casually waylay him, on some remote Mediterranean road . . . How desperate are you? Enough to shove Luke off a convenient cliff? Yes? No? What's that horrible thing you are knitting? A scarf? It looks lethal! Is it to strangle Luke with?"

"Oh, shut up!" said Caddy, but she did not stop knitting the scarf. Rose inspected it from time to time, and then went and gloated over a small box she was taking care of for Michael. It was supposed to be a total secret, and almost was, except that she could not resist sharing it with Indigo.

"Promise you won't tell anyone?"

"Promise."

"Not even Tom?"

"Oh, all right."

Tom and Indigo were in constant contact again. Several times a week they e-mailed each other, exchanging news, music, guitar playing advice, and the occasional chunk of *Le Morte D'Arthur.*

"What does Tom make of all that stuff?" asked David one day, watching as Indigo typed, 'And so Bagdemagus departed and did many adventures and proved after a full good knight.'

"Thinks it's fantastic," said Indigo.

"I think it's rubbish," grumbled David, and read over Indigo's shoulder,

And so on the morn . . .
there fell,
New tidings
And other adventures.

"Tell him I'm getting drumming lessons for Christmas," said David, and Indigo smiled.

"And one day I'm getting a set of drums and Granddad says I can keep it at his house when I do."

“One day we’ll have a band,” said Indigo.

“Who will?” asked Rose, coming in just then.

“David and Tom and me.”

“What about me?”

“And you. Any messages for Tom, Rosy Pose?”

“Oh,” said Rose, “just tell him I’m still here.”

“Nothing else you want to say?”

“Nothing that matters,” said Rose.

The new computer that made all this possible had been bought by Bill. He had bought a number of very expensive presents lately.

“Guilt,” said Saffron.

It had taken Saffron a long time to recover from the shock of discovering who her father was. It would have taken even longer if it had not been for Sarah. Sarah loyally listened and sympathized through all the tears and anger.

“Good thing,” Sarah said when they at last reached the point of being able to joke again, “that we spent the summer cultivating hearts of stone.”

Bill did guilt as beautifully as he did everything else. Humble. Gentle. Making no excuses. Saying (as he flicked a speck of dust from his sleeve) (“He is not cool with dust," remarked Sarah), "I shall never forgive myself. Never. Saffy darling."

Saffron had been so horrible to him then that she felt guilty afterward.

"He still smiles the same smile," said Sarah, consoling her.

Eve forgave Bill very easily, having had plenty of practice at this in the past. "Anyway," she said, "I suppose I always knew. Or could have known, if I'd wanted to. Poor darling Linda . . ."

"Do you really not hate her?" asked Saffron.

"Of course I don't! Of *course* I don't! And never did, and never will, not for a moment! I *do* understand," said Eve, and added dreamily. "We always did share everything!"

"Eve!" said Sarah.

"And after all, it was Linda who knew Bill first!"

Eve smiled at them lovingly, kissed Rose, and wandered out to her shed. Saffron and Sarah looked at each other, and each could see the other's eyes were fizzing with a dozen questions.

"Saint, or just more or less totally bonkers?" asked Sarah at last. "Probably which?"

"I think probably both," said Saffron.

Then nobody said anything for a long time until Indigo came in. He had brought a message that had just come to Rose from Tom.

"It looked so good I printed it out for you," he said as he handed it over.

It was beautiful, giant rainbow letters:

HELLO,

PERMANENT ROSE!

Rose was so pleased with it, she took it out to the shed, where she and Eve admired it together.

"Perfect!" said Eve. "Isn't it?"

"Perfect," agreed Rose, and then she asked, "Why did you call me that? Why did you? *Did* you mean it for a joke?"

"No," said Eve at once. "No, Rosy Pose. Really . . . I really meant it for . . ."

"What? Tell me."

"A promise," said Eve.

Here's a peek at the next book about the Casson family:

CADDY EVER AFTER

THE FLYING FEELING

by Rose Casson

Class 4

TODAY I FELL ASLEEP IN CLASS. SCHOOL HAD HARDLY BEGUN (it was Literacy Hour). Miss Farley, my class teacher, touched me on my shoulder to wake me up.

"NO NO," I shouted very loudly, and fell on the floor and crawled under the table to escape.

Then I realized where I was, so I came out and sat down again as quietly as I could. I hoped that if I was quick and quiet enough Miss Farley almost would not notice I had done anything unusual. But she did.

Miss Farley said, "Rose, is there anything wrong? Here at school? Or at home, perhaps?"

I could tell by the way she looked at me that she had not forgotten about yesterday.

WHY I FELL ASLEEP IN CLASS
A LONG THOUGHT

MISS FARLEY HAS A BIG CHEEK ASKING ME IF THERE IS anything wrong like that. In front of everyone. How would she like it if I did it to her? On one of those days when she comes in with little eyes and no lipstick and snaps, "Right Class 4, we will separate these groups of tables into lines, since you cannot seem to behave as you are! Rose Casson, what is so interesting out of that window?" (sky) "Also, Rose, since when have tie-dyed T-shirts been school uniform, may I ask? And before you do anything, go to the office and take out that earring and ask them for a recycled envelope to put it in, please."

On those days, do I ask, "Miss Farley, is there anything wrong at home? Or at school, perhaps?"

No.

Luckily, she has not noticed my earring today. It is a gold hoop with dangling red crystals on gold links. My sister Saffron gave it to me this morning.

There is a clean patch on the carpet in the reading corner where one of the carpet squares has been shampooed. So nobody in the class can forget about yesterday either.

Also Ghost Club has been banned.

GHOST CLUB

ON RAINY LUNCH BREAKS AT OUR SCHOOL YOU CAN EITHER GO to the hall and play, or stay in your classroom and be as quiet as mice. (If mice are like hamsters they are not very quiet.) That is when we do Ghost Club, Kiran (who used to be my best friend) and me and some of the others.

For Ghost Club we turn off the lights and pull down the blinds as far as they will go and sit in a circle on the floor, on the carpet squares in the reading corner. Then we very, very quietly, very quietly, really quietly take turns to tell ghost stories.

Yesterday was a rainy day, and so we did Ghost Club. First Molly told us about her grandad whose false teeth slid out when he fell asleep watching football.

"I don't think that sounds very scary," I said.

"Yes, well, okay it is only slightly scary," agreed Molly, "but admit it is totally gross!"

I admitted this at once, and then I told about the strange scratchy noises in our house at night, which cannot be my sister Caddy's escaped hamsters because they would have died ages ago. According to the hamster book.

Everyone at Ghost Club said their houses made strange noises at night too, which their mothers told them were caused by central heating. I explained that we did not have central heating.

Kiran hummed like she was bored and picked at a carpet square and said, "All houses creak a bit and you can get false tooth glue to keep them in, they advertise it on daytime TV when they know old people are watching. You know my cousin? No, carry on talking about central heating! Maybe I shouldn't tell you!"

So of course we made her tell us.

Kiran's stories are the worst because they are true. They are all about people in her family.

I used to think, thank goodness I am not related to Kiran. If I was related to Kiran I would not feel safe.

Terrible things happen all the time to that family.

"Which cousin?" we asked Kiran, because her family (as well as being unsafe) is enormous.

"My cousin who doesn't go to this school with the pink jacket," Kiran told us. "You know that one?"

"No," we said.

"Well, you know my Auntie who came on visitor's day who had to have all the windows opened very quickly?"

"Yes," we said.

"That's her mother. She bought my cousin the pink jacket. From the market stall next to the mobile ear piercing van. And anyway, you know that place by the park near Rose's house where no one is allowed to go?"

"No," we said.

"Yes you do, it is all fenced in and a notice says DANGER HIGH VOLTAGE."

"It is an electricity substation," said Molly, who always knows stuff like that because she goes on Intelligent Quality Time walks with her mother. (I don't.)

"Well," continued Kiran very quickly, before Molly could start telling us about substations, "my cousin with the pink jacket was walking past that place and it was winter and it was nearly dark and you know how if you hold your hand up very close to your face and it is nearly dark, all the fingers look thick and black and not real?"

We said no, and then we tried it with our own hands sitting in the nearly-darkness of the reading corner, and then we said, "Oh yes."

"A hand like that but much bigger," said Kiran. She was speaking very quietly indeed now, like she did not really want us to hear. "Over her shoulder. And no footprints. No sound of footprints. And not quite touching her. My cousin. And the fingers very thick and dark like a thick dark leather glove. Not smooth leather. Reaching over her shoulder, just at that place by the park where you are not allowed to go. She saw it out of the corner of her eye."

Nobody said anything.

"She just caught sight of it for a moment. The first time."

You could hear the clock, and the sound of people being told off in the hall and you could hear us breathing.

"But she saw it for longer the next time."

"Did she look around?" whispered Molly.

"Only once."

"What did she see?"

"She won't tell me."

"Ki . . . raaan!" we wailed.

"So now she won't wear her pink jacket and my Auntie says it is a waste because it was nearly new and she says I can have it and wear it with a scarf. Because they won't wash off; they are burnt on."

"*WHAT* ARE BURNT ON?" shouted several people.

"The finger marks," said Kiran, sounding very surprised that we did not know. "The thick burnt brown finger marks on the shoulder of the jacket."

We didn't say anything.

"I don't want that revolting jacket," said Kiran.

Still nobody said anything. We were thinking. We knew the place by the park where you are not allowed to go. We knew Kiran's Auntie who bought the jacket, and we knew the market stall it came from. We even knew the mobile ear piercing van; my sister Saffron had her nose pierced there. When I thought about it, I thought I even knew Kiran's cousin who doesn't go to this school. And I knew, exactly as if I had seen them, what the thick dark finger marks looked like scorched onto the shoulder of that pink jacket.

Someone grabbed my shoulder very hard and shouted, "ROSE'S TURN!"

I jumped so badly I felt sick and dizzy and I shouted, "Not me!" without even meaning to shout, but I don't think it sounded very loud. Everyone was laughing so much.

Kiran said, "I am sorry Rose, I am sorry Rose, I am sorry Rose!" but I will never forgive her.

If I had a choice between dying and wetting myself in class, I would choose dying.

HAMSTERS

These are the people who live at my house:

1. Me.
2. Mummy, who is called Eve. She is an artist. She does her art in a shed at the bottom of the garden. It is not true that Mummy calls everyone darling to save her bothering to remember names.
3. Indigo, who is my brother and is five years older than me. Indigo is very tall and thin. With his eyes closed he looks dead. He always has, but no one has ever got used to it. This is bad luck for Indigo. It means that ever since he was a baby frightened people have been shaking him awake to make sure

he is still alive. Over the years Indigo has grown more and more difficult to wake up.

4. Saffron. She is really my cousin, but she is my adopted sister too. She is nearly fifteen and she is very pretty (like Caddy) and very clever (like Indigo). When Saffron found out about yesterday at Ghost Club she said, "One way of getting the carpet cleaned, Rosy Pose!"

Saffron is ruthless.

These are the people who do not live at my house:

1. Daddy. He lives in London where he has a studio. Because he is an artist too. (He says.)
2. My grown-up sister Caddy who is at university. Before she went to university she kept more guinea pigs and hamsters than most people would want to own. She kept them all over the place. There are still some guinea pigs left in a hutch in the garden, but the hamsters are all gone.

But where have they gone?

• • •

Yesterday evening when my sister Saffron was doing her homework and my brother Indigo was lying on the floor listening to terrible music with his headphones on (this is still about why I fell asleep in class) I told Mummy what happened at school. She was making an illuminated manuscript because she is having a display of illuminated manuscripts in the library. Poems in old-fashioned writing with little pictures around the capital letters and decorated edges. On this poem she was drawing singing birds, all different bright colors among the leaves.

"I know darling Bill would say it is Not Exactly Art," she said (Darling Bill is Daddy). "But it is fun and they sell amazingly well and the suspension on my car has more or less gone completely. These days it is more like sledging along on your bottom than real driving so I will have to get it fixed and goodness knows what it will cost. Do you like the poem, Rosy Pose? It is tenth-century Irish. Translated. Caddy used to have accidents at school so often that I put dry knickers in every morning with her packed lunch. Until she started school dinners."

Then there was a big bang and all the lights went out.

• • •

"Goodness," said Mummy after a minute or two. "Or is it just one bulb?"

Indigo continued to lie on the floor with his eyes shut, droning away to his terrible music because he was running on batteries.

"No, it isn't just one bulb," said Mummy, futilely flicking switches. "It is all over the house." Then she accidentally trod on Indigo and he unplugged himself and said, "Candles."

"I know," said Mummy. "But unfortunately not. I threw them all away after I had a terrible dream about Rose accidentally setting the house on fire. In case it was a warning. And I took that big cinnamon scented one in to college to relax my Young Offenders only last week . . ." (Mummy teaches Art to Young Offenders so that they can do their vandalizing with style and confidence (Daddy says).) ". . . and it is still there. I wonder if the power is off in the shed?"

Indigo said he would go and see and he went outside and did and it wasn't, because the shed was properly wired by an intelligent hippy who lived in a tent and who (briefly) fell in love with Caddy and then Mummy. He unblocked the sink too. But soon

after that he went to Tangier in an old bus. His name was Derek, and he would have taken Mummy to Tangier with him, and me and Indy and Saffron too, and Caddy could have visited for holidays. There was plenty of room in the bus. But we didn't go. Because Mummy said, "What about darling Bill?"

And Derek said there wasn't that much room in the bus.

What has this got to do with why I fell asleep in class?

Everything.

But what has it got to do with hamsters?

We didn't find out till morning.

Mummy said, "Oh good, that solves everything!" when she heard there was still power in the shed.

Mummy would be perfectly happy to live in the shed.